Nora Roberts is the *New York Times* bestselling author of more than one hundred and ninety novels. A born storyteller, she creates a blend of warmth, humour and poignancy that speaks directly to her readers and has earned her almost every award for excellence in her field. The youngest of five children, Nora Roberts lives in western Maryland. She has two sons.

Visit her website at www.noraroberts.com

Nora Roberts

Secret Star

MILLS &
BOON

HarperCollins
PUBLISHERS
—— Since 1817 ——

This edition published in Great Britain 2017
By Mills & Boon, an imprint of HarperCollins*Publishers*
1 London Bridge Street, London, SE1 9GF

Secret Star © 1998 Nora Roberts

ISBN: 978-0-263-92746-7

29-0417

Our policy is to use papers that are natural, renewable and recyclable products and made from wood grown in sustainable forests. The logging and manufacturing processes conform to the legal environmental regulations of the country of origin.

Printed and bound
by CPI Group (UK) Ltd, Croydon, CRO 4YY

To generous hearts

Chapter 1

The woman in the portrait had a face created to steal a man's breath and haunt his dreams. It was, perhaps, as close to perfection as nature would allow. Eyes of laser blue whispered of sex and smiled knowingly from beneath thick black lashes. The brows were perfectly arched, with a flirty little mole dotting the downward point of the left one. The skin was porcelain-pure, with a hint of warm rose beneath—just warm enough that a man could fantasize that heat was kindling only for him. The nose was straight and finely sculpted.

The mouth—and, oh, the mouth was hard to ignore—was curved invitingly, appeared pillow-soft, yet strong in shape. A bold red temptation that beckoned as clearly as a siren's call.

Framing that staggering face was a rich, wild tumble

of ebony hair that streamed over creamy bare shoulders. Glossy, gorgeous, generous. The kind of hair even a strong man would lose himself in—fisting his hands in all that black silk, while his mouth sank deep, and deeper, into those soft, smiling lips.

Grace Fontaine, Seth thought, a study in the perfection of feminine beauty.

It was too damn bad she was dead.

He turned away from the portrait, annoyed that his gaze and his mind kept drifting back to it. He'd wanted some time alone at the crime scene, after the forensic team finished, after the M.E. took possession of the body. The outline remained, an ugly human-shaped silhouette marring the glossy chestnut floor.

It was simple enough to determine how she'd died. A nasty tumble from the floor above, right through the circling railing, now splintered and sharp-edged, and down, beautiful face first, into the lake-size glass table.

She'd lost her beauty in death, he thought, and that was a damn shame, too.

It was also simple to determine that she'd been given some help with that last dive.

It was, he mused, looking around, a terrific house. The high ceilings offered space and half a dozen generous skylights gave light, rosy, hopeful beams from the dying sun. Everything curved—the stairs, the doorways, the windows. Female again, he supposed. The wood was glossy, the glass sparkling, the furniture all obviously carefully selected antiques.

Someone was going to have a tough time getting the bloodstains out of the dove-gray upholstery of the sofa.

He tried to imagine how it had all looked before whoever helped Grace Fontaine off the balcony stormed through the rooms.

There wouldn't have been broken statuary or ripped cushions. Flowers would have been meticulously arranged in vases, rather than crushed into the intricate pattern of the Oriental rugs.

There certainly wouldn't have been blood, broken glass, or layers of fingerprint dust.

She'd lived well, he thought. But then, she had been able to afford to live well. She'd become an heiress when she turned twenty-one, the privileged, pampered orphan and the wild child of the Fontaine empire. An excellent education, a country-club darling, and the headache, he imagined, of the conservative and staunch Fontaines, of Fontaine Department Stores fame.

Rarely had a week gone by that Grace Fontaine didn't warrant a mention in the society pages of the *Washington Post,* or a paparazzi shot in one of the glossies. And it usually hadn't been due to a good deed.

The press would be screaming with this latest, and last, adventure in the life and times of Grace Fontaine, Seth knew, the moment the news leaked. And they would be certain to mention all of her escapades. Posing nude at nineteen for a centerfold spread, the steamy and very public affair with a very married English lord, the dalliance with a hot heartthrob from Hollywood.

There'd been other notches in her designer belt, Seth remembered. A United States senator, a bestselling author, the artist who had painted her portrait, the rock star who, rumor had it, had attempted to take his own life when she dumped him.

She'd packed a lot of men into a short life.

Grace Fontaine was dead at twenty-six.

It was his job to find out not only the how, but the who. And the why.

He had a line on the why already. The Three Stars of Mithra—a fortune in blue diamonds, the impulsive and desperate act of a friend, and greed.

Seth frowned as he walked through the empty house, cataloging the events that had brought him to this place, to this point. Since he had a personal interest in mythology, had since childhood, he knew something about the Three Stars. They were the stuff of legends, and had once been grouped in a gold triangle that had been held in the hands of a statue of the god Mithra.

One stone for love, he remembered, skimming through details as he climbed the curved stairs to the second level. One for knowledge, and the last for generosity. Mythologically speaking, whoever possessed the Stars gained the god's power. And immortality.

Which was, logically, a crock, of course. Wasn't it odd, though, he mused, that he'd been dreaming lately of flashing blue stones, a dark castle shrouded in mist, a room of glinting gold? And there was a man with eyes as pale as death, he thought, trying to clear the hazy details. And a woman with the face of a goddess.

And his own violent death.

Seth shook off the uneasy sensation that accompanied his recalling the snippets of dreams. What he required now were facts, basic, logical facts. And the fact was that three blue diamonds weighing something over a hundred carats apiece were worth six kings' ransoms. And someone wanted them, and didn't mind killing to gain possession.

He had bodies piling up like cordwood, he thought, dragging a hand through his dark hair. In order of death, the first had been Thomas Salvini, part owner of Salvini, gem experts who had been contracted by the Smithsonian Institution to verify and assess the three stones. Evidence pointed to the fact that verifying and assessing hadn't been quite enough for Thomas Salvini, or his twin, Timothy.

Over a million in cash indicated that they'd had other plans—and a client who wanted the Stars for himself.

Added to that was the statement from one Bailey

James, the Salvinis' stepsister, and eyewitness to fratricide. A gemologist with an impeccable reputation, she claimed to have discovered her stepbrothers' plans to copy the stones, sell the originals and leave the country with the profits.

She'd gone in to see her brothers alone, he thought with a shake of his head. Without contacting the police. And she'd decided to face them down after she shipped two of the stones to her two closest friends, separating them to protect them. He gave a short sigh at the mysterious minds of civilians.

Well, she'd paid for her impulse, he thought. Walking in on a vicious murder, barely escaping with her life—and with her memory of the incident and everything before it blocked for days.

He stepped into Grace's bedroom, his heavy-lidded gold-toned eyes cooly scanning the brutally searched room.

And had Bailey James gone to the police even then? No, she'd chosen a P.I., right out of the phone book. Seth's mouth thinned in annoyance. He had very little respect and no admiration for private investigators. Through blind luck, she'd stumbled across a fairly decent one, he acknowledged. Cade Parris wasn't as bad as most, and he'd managed—through more blind luck, Seth was certain—to sniff out a trail.

And nearly gotten himself killed in the process.

Which brought Seth to death number two. Timothy Salvini was now as dead as his brother. He couldn't blame Parris overmuch for defending himself from a man with a knife, but taking the second Salvini out left a dead end.

And through the eventful Fourth of July weekend, Bailey James's other friend had been on the run with a bounty hunter. In a rare show of outward emotion, Seth rubbed his eyes and leaned against the door jamb.

M. J. O'Leary. He'd be interviewing her soon, personally. And he'd be the one telling her, and Bailey James, that their friend Grace was dead. Both tasks fell under his concept of duty.

O'Leary had the second Star and had been underground with the skip tracer, Jack Dakota, since Saturday afternoon. Though it was only Monday evening now, M.J. and her companion had managed to rack up a number of points—including three more bodies.

Seth reflected on the foolish and unsavory bail bondsman who'd not only set Dakata up with the false job of bringing in M.J., but also moonlighted with blackmail. The hired muscle who'd been after M.J. had likely been part of some scam of his and had killed him. Then they'd had some very bad luck on a rain-slicked road.

And that left him with yet another dead end.

Grace Fontaine was likely to be third. He wasn't certain what her empty house, her mangled possessions, would tell him. He would, however, go through it all, inch by inch and step by step. That was his style.

He would be thorough, he would be careful, and he would find the answers. He believed in order, he believed in laws. He believed, unstintingly, in justice.

Seth Buchanan was a third-generation cop, and had worked his way up the rank to lieutenant due to an inherent skill for police work, an almost terrifying patience, and a hard-edged objectivity. The men under him respected him—some secretly feared him. He was well aware he was often referred to as the Machine, and took no offense. Emotion, temperament, the grief and the guilt civilians could indulge in, had no place in the job.

If he was considered aloof, even cold and controlled, he saw it as a compliment.

He stood a moment longer in the doorway, the mahogany-framed mirror across the wide room reflecting him. He was a tall, well-built man, muscles toned to iron under a dark suit jacket. He'd loosened his tie because he was alone, and his nightwing hair was slightly disordered by the rake of his fingers. It was full and thick, with a slight wave. He pushed it back from an unsmiling face that boasted a square jaw and tawny skin.

His nose had been broken years before, when he was

in uniform, and it edged his face toward the rugged. His mouth was hard, firm, and rare to smile. His eyes, the dark gold of an old painting, remained cool under straight black brows.

On one wide-palmed hand he wore the ring that had been his father's. On either side of the heavy gold were the words *Serve* and *Protect*.

He took both duties seriously.

Bending, he picked up a pool of red silk that had been tossed on the mountain of scattered clothing heaped on the Aubusson carpet. The callused tips of his fingers skimmed over it. The red silk gown matched the short robe the victim had been wearing, he thought.

He wanted to think of her only as the victim, not as the woman in the portrait, certainly not as the woman in those new and disturbing dreams that disrupted his sleep. And he was irritated that his mind kept swimming back to that stunning face—the woman behind it. That quality was—had been, he corrected—part of her power. That skill in drilling into a man's mind until he was obsessed with her.

She would have been irresistible, he mused, still holding the wisp of silk. Unforgettable. Dangerous.

Had she slipped into that little swirl of silk for a man? he wondered. Had she been expecting company—a private evening of passion?

And where was the third Star? Had her unexpected

visitor found it, taken it? The safe in the library downstairs had been broken open, cleaned out. It seemed
logical that she would have locked something that valu-
able away. Yet she'd taken the fall from up here.

Had she run? Had he chased her? Why had she let
him in the house? The sturdy locks on the doors hadn't
been tampered with. Had she been careless, reckless
enough to open the door to a stranger while she wore
nothing but a thin silk robe?

Or had she known him?

Perhaps she'd bragged about the diamond, even
shown it off to him. Had greed taken the place of
passion? An argument, then a fight. A struggle, a fall.
Then the destruction of the house as cover.

It was an avenue, he decided. He had her thick address book downstairs, and would go through it name
by name. Just as he, and the team he assigned, would
go through the empty house in Potomac, Maryland,
inch by inch.

But he had people to see now. Tragedy to spread and
details to tie up. He would have to ask one of Grace
Fontaine's friends, or a member of her family, to come
in and officially identify the body.

He regretted, more than he wanted to, that anyone
who had cared for her would have to look at that ruined face.

He let the silk gown drop, took one last look at the

room, with its huge bed and trampled flowers, the scatter of lovely old antique bottles that gleamed like precious gems. He already knew that the scent here would haunt him, just as that perfect face painted beautifully in oils in the room downstairs would.

It was full dark when he returned. It wasn't unusual for him to put long, late hours into a case. Seth had no life to speak of outside of the job, had never sought to make one. The women he saw socially, or romantically, were carefully, even calculatingly, selected. Most tolerated the demands of his work poorly, and they rarely cemented a relationship. Because he knew how difficult and frustrating those demands of time, energy and heart were on those who waited, he expected complaints, sulking, even accusations, from the women who felt neglected.

So he never made promises. And he lived alone.

He knew there was little he could do here at the scene. He should have been at his desk—or at least, he thought, have gone home just to let his mind clear. But he'd been pulled back to this house. No, to this woman, he admitted. It wasn't the two stories of wood and glass, however lovely, that dragged at him.

It was the face in the portrait.

He'd left his car at the top of the sweep of the drive, and walked to the house sheltered by grand old trees and well-trimmed shrubs green with summer. He'd let himself in, turned the switch that had the foyer chandelier blazing light.

His men had already started the tedious door-to-door of the neighborhood, hoping that someone, in another of the big, exquisite homes, would have heard something, seen anything.

The medical examiner was slow—understandably, Seth reminded himself. It was a holiday, and the staff was down to bare minimum. Official reports would take a bit longer.

But it wasn't the reports or lack of them that nagged at his mind as he wandered back, inevitably, to the portrait over the glazed-tile hearth.

Grace Fontaine had been loved. He'd underestimated the depth friendship could reach. But he'd seen that depth, and that shocked and racking grief in the faces of the two women he'd just left.

There had been a bond between Bailey James, M. J. O'Leary and Grace that was as strong as he'd ever seen. He regretted—and he rarely had regrets— that he'd had to tell them so bluntly.

I'm sorry for your loss.

Words cops said to euphemize the death they lived with—often violent, always unexpected. He had said the words, as he had too often in the past, and watched the fragile blonde and the cat-eyed redhead simply crumble. Clutching each other, they had simply crumbled. 1078, 096 AFP

He hadn't needed the two men who had ranged themselves as the women's champions to tell him to leave them alone with their grief. There would be no questions, no statements, no answers, that night. Nothing he could say or do would penetrate that thick curtain of grief.

Grace Fontaine had been loved, he thought again, looking into those spectacular blue eyes. Not simply desired by men, but loved by two women. What was behind those eyes, what was behind that face, that had deserved that kind of unquestioning emotion?

"Who the hell were you?" he murmured, and was answered by that bold, inviting smile. "Too beautiful to be real. Too aware of your own beauty to be soft." His deep voice, rough with fatigue, echoed in the empty house. He slipped his hands in his pockets, rocked back on his heels. "Too dead to care."

And though he turned from the portrait, he had the uneasy feeling that it was watching him. Measuring him.

He had yet to reach her next of kin, the aunt and uncle in Virginia who had raised her after the death of her parents. The aunt was summering in a villa in Italy and was, for tonight, out of touch.

Villas in Italy, he mused, blue diamonds, oil portraits

over fireplaces of sapphire-blue tile. It was a world far removed from his firmly middle-class upbringing, and from the life he'd embraced through his career.

But he knew violence didn't play favorites.

He would eventually go home to his tiny little house on its postage-stamp lot, crowded together with dozens of other tiny little houses. It would be empty, as he'd never found a woman who moved him to want to share even that small private space. But his home would be there for him.

And this house, for all its gleaming wood and acres of gleaming glass, its sloping lawn, sparkling pool and trimmed bushes, hadn't protected its mistress.

He walked around the stark outline on the floor and started up the stairs again. His mood was edgy—he could admit that. And the best thing to smooth it out again was work.

He thought perhaps a woman with as eventful a life as Grace Fontaine would have noted those events—and her personal feelings about them—in a diary.

He worked in silence, going through her bedroom carefully, knowing very well that he was trapped in that sultry scent she'd left behind.

He'd taken his tie off, tucked it in his pocket. The weight from his weapon, snug in his shoulder harness, was so much a part of him it went unnoticed.

He went through her drawers without a qualm,

though they were largely empty now, as their contents were strewn around the room. He searched beneath them, behind them and under the mattress.

He thought, irrelevantly, that she'd owned enough clothing to outfit a good-size modeling troupe, and that she'd leaned toward soft materials. Silks, cashmeres, satins, thin brushed wools. Bold colors. Jewel colors, with a bent toward blues.

With those eyes, he thought as they crept back into his mind, why not?

He caught himself wondering how her voice had sounded. Would it have fit that sultry face, been husky and low, another purr of temptation for a man? He imagined it that way, a voice as dark and sensual as the scent that hung on the air.

Her body had fit the face, fit the scent, he mused, stepping into her enormous walk-in closet. Of course, she'd helped nature along there. And he wondered why a woman would feel impelled to add silicone to her body to lure a man. And what kind of pea-brained man would prefer it to an honest shape.

He preferred honesty in women. Insisted on it. Which, he supposed, was one of the reasons he lived alone.

He scanned the clothes still hanging with a shake of his head. Even the killer had run out of patience here, it seemed. The hangers were swept back so that garments were crowded together, but he hadn't bothered to pull them all out.

Seth judged that the number of shoes totaled well over two hundred, and one wall of shelves had obviously been fashioned to hold handbags. These, in every imaginable shape and size and color, had been pulled out of their slots, ripped open and searched.

A cupboard had held more—sweaters, scarves. Costume jewelry. He imagined she'd had plenty of the real sparkles, as well. Some would have been in the now empty safe downstairs, he was sure. And she might have a lockbox at a bank.

That he would check on first thing in the morning.

She'd enjoyed music, he mused, scanning the wireless speakers. He'd seen speakers in every room of the house, and there had been CDs, tapes, even old albums, tossed around the living area downstairs. She'd had eclectic taste there. Everything from Bach to the B-52s.

Had she spent many evenings alone? he wondered. With music playing through the house? Had she ever curled up in front of that classy fireplace with one of the hundreds of books that lined the walls of her library?

Snuggled up on the couch, he thought, wearing that little red robe, with her million-dollar legs tucked up. A glass of brandy, the music on low, the starlight streaming through the roof windows.

He could see it too well. He could see her look up, skim that fall of hair back from that staggering face, curve those tempting lips as she caught him watching her. Set the book aside, reach out a hand in invitation, give that low, husky purr of a laugh as she drew him down beside her.

He could almost taste it.

Because he could, he swore under his breath, gave himself a moment to control the sudden upbeat of his heart rate.

Dead or alive, he decided, the woman was a witch. And the damn stones, preposterous or not, only seemed to add to her power.

And he was wasting his time. Completely wasting it, he told himself as he rose. He was covering ground best covered through rules and routine. He needed to go back, light a fire under the M.E., push for an estimated time of death. He needed to start calling the numbers in the victim's address book.

He needed to get out of this house that smelled of this woman. All but breathed of her. And stay out of it, he determined, until he was certain he could rein in his uncharacteristic imaginings.

Annoyed with himself, irked by his own deviation from strict routine, he walked back through the bedroom. He'd just started down the curve of the stairs when a movement caught his eye. His hand reached for his weapon. But it was already too late for that.

Very slowly, he dropped his hand, stood where he was and stared down. It wasn't the automatic pointed at his heart that stunned him motionless. It was the fact that it was held, steady as a rock, in the hand of a dead woman.

"Well," the dead woman said, stepping forward into the halo of light from the foyer chandelier. "You're certainly a messy thief, and a stupid one." Those shockingly blue eyes stared up at him. "Why don't you give me one good reason why I shouldn't put a hole in your head before I call the police?"

For a ghost, she met his earlier fantasy perfectly. The voice was a purr, hot and husky and stunningly alive. And for the recently departed, she had a very warm flush of temper in her cheeks. It wasn't often that Seth's mind clicked off. But it had. He saw a woman, runway-fresh in white silk, the glint of jewels at her ears and a shiny silver gun in her hand.

He pulled himself back roughly, though none of the shock or the effort showed as he met her demand with an unsmiling response. "I *am* the police."

Her lips curved, a generous bow of sarcasm. "Of course you are, handsome. Who else would be creeping around a locked house when no one's at home but an overworked cop on his beat?"

"I haven't been a beat cop for quite some time. I'm Buchanan. Lieutenant Seth Buchanan. If you'd aim your weapon just a little to the left of my heart, I'll show you my badge."

"I'd just love to see it." Watching him, she slowly shifted the barrel of the gun. Her heart was thudding like a jackhammer with a combination of fear and anger, but she took another casual step forward as he reached two fingers into his pocket. The badge looked real enough, she mused. What she could see of the identification with the gold shield on the flap that he held up.

And she began to get a very bad feeling. A worse sinking in the stomach sensation than she'd experienced when she pulled up to the drive, saw the strange car and the lights blazing inside her empty house.

She flicked her eyes from the badge up to his again. Damned if he didn't look more like a cop than a crook, she decided. Very attractive, in a straight-edged, buttoned-down sort of fashion. The solid body, broad of shoulder and narrow of hip, appeared ruthlessly disciplined.

Eyes like that, cool and clear and golden brown, that seemed to see everything at once, belonged to either a cop or a criminal. Either way, she imagined, they belonged to a dangerous sort of man.

Dangerous men usually appealed to her. But at the

moment, as she took in the oddity of the situation, her mood wasn't receptive.

"All right, Buchanan, Lieutenant Seth, why don't you tell me what you're doing in my house." She thought of what she carried in her purse—what Bailey had sent her only days before—and felt that unsettling sensation in her stomach deepen.

What kind of trouble are we in? she wondered. And just how do I slide out of it with a cop staring me down?

"Have you got a search warrant to go along with that badge?" she demanded.

"No, I don't." He'd have felt better, considerably better, if she'd put the gun down altogether. But she seemed content to hold it, aiming it lower now, no less steadily, but lower. Still, his composure had snapped back. Keeping his eyes on hers, he came down the rest of the stairs and stood in the lofty foyer, facing her. "You're Grace Fontaine."

She watched him tuck his badge back into his pocket, while those unreadable cop's eyes skimmed over her face. Memorizing features, she thought, irritated. Making mental note of any distinguishing marks. Just what the hell was going on?

"Yes, I'm Grace Fontaine. This is my property, my home. And as you're in it, without a proper warrant, you're trespassing. As calling a cop seems superfluous, maybe I'll just call my lawyer."

He angled his head, and unwillingly caught a whiff of that siren's scent of hers. Perhaps it was that, and feeling its instant and unwelcome effect on his system, that had him speaking without thought.

"Well, Ms. Fontaine, you look damn good for a dead woman."

Chapter 2

Her response was to narrow her eyes, arch a brow. "If that's some sort of cop humor, I'm afraid you'll have to translate."

It annoyed him that she'd jarred the remark out of him. It wasn't professional. Cautious, he brought a hand up slowly, tipped the barrel of the gun farther to the left. "Do you mind?" he said, then, quickly, before she could agree, he twisted it neatly out of her hand, pulled out the clip. It wasn't the time to ask if she had a license to carry, so he merely handed her back the empty gun and pocketed the clip.

"It's best to keep both hands on your weapon," he said easily, and with such sobriety that she suspected amusement lurked beneath. "And, if you want to keep it, not to get within reach."

"Thanks so much for the lesson in self-defense." Obviously irritated, she opened her bag and dumped the gun inside. "But you still haven't answered my initial question, Lieutenant. Why are you in my house?"

"You've had an incident, Ms. Fontaine."

"An incident? More copspeak?" She blew out a breath. "Was there a break-in?" she asked, and for the first time took her attention off the man and glanced past him into the foyer. "A robbery?" she added, then caught sight of an overturned chair and some smashed crockery through the archway in the living area.

Swearing, she started to push past him. He curled a hand over her arm to stop her. "Ms. Fontaine—"

"Get your hand off me," she snapped, interrupting him. "This is my home."

He kept his grip firm. "I'm aware of that. Exactly when was the last time you were in it?"

"I'll give you a damn statement after I've seen what's missing." She managed another two steps and saw from the disorder in the living area that it hadn't been a neat or organized robbery. "Well, they did quite a job, didn't they? My cleaning service is going to be very unhappy."

She glanced down to where Seth's fingers were still curled around her arm. "Are you testing my biceps, Lieutenant? I do like to think they're firm."

"Your muscle tone's fine." From what he could see

of her in the filmy ivory slacks, it appeared more than fine. "I'd like you to answer my question, Ms. Fontaine. When were you home last?"

"Here?" She sighed, shrugged one elegant shoulder. Her mind was flitting around the annoying details that were the backwash of a robbery. Calling her insurance agent, filing a claim, giving statements. "Wednesday afternoon. I went out of town for a few days." She was more shaken than she cared to admit that her house had been robbed and ransacked in her absence. Her things touched and taken by strangers. But she slid him a smiling glance from under her lashes. "Aren't you going to take notes?"

"As a matter of fact, I am. Shortly. Who was staying in the house in your absence?"

"No one. I don't care to have people in my home when I'm away. Now if you'll excuse me…" She gave her arm a quick, hard jerk and strode through the foyer and under the arch. "Good God." The anger came first, quick and intense. She wanted to kick something, no matter that it was broken and ruined already. "Did they have to break what they didn't cart out?" she muttered. She glanced up, saw the splintered railing and swore again. "And what the devil did they do up there? A lot of good an alarm system does if anyone can just…"

She stopped her forward motion, her voice trailing off, as she saw the outline on the gleaming chestnut wood of the floor. As she stared at it, unable to tear her eyes away, the blood drained out of her face, leaving it painfully cold and stiff.

Placing one hand on the back of the stained sofa for balance, she stared down at the outline, the diamond glitter of broken glass that had been her coffee table, and the blood that had dried to a dark pool.

"Why don't we go into the dining room?" he said quietly.

She jerked her shoulders back, though he hadn't touched her. The pit of her stomach was cased in ice, and the flashes of heat that lanced through her did nothing to melt it. "Who was killed?" she demanded. "Who died here?"

"Up until a few minutes ago, it was assumed you did."

She closed her eyes, vaguely concerned that her vision was dimming at the edges. "Excuse me," she said, quite clearly, and walked across the room on numb legs. She picked up a bottle of brandy that lay on its side on the floor, fumbled open a display cabinet for a glass. And poured generously.

She took the first drink as medicine. He could see that in the way she tossed it back, shuddered twice, hard. It didn't bring the color back to her face, but he imagined it had shocked her system into functioning again.

"Ms. Fontaine, I think it would be better if we talked about this in another room."

"I'm all right." But her voice was raw. She drank again before turning to him. "Why did you think it was me?"

"The victim was in your house, dressed in a robe. She met your general description. Her face had been… damaged by the fall. She was your approximate height and weight, your age, your coloring."

Her coloring, Grace thought on a wave of staggering relief. Not Bailey or M.J., then. "I had no houseguest while I was gone." She took a deep breath, knowing the calm was there, if only she could reach it. "I have no idea who the woman was, unless it was one of the burglars. How did she—" Grace looked up again at the broken railing, the viciously sharp edges of wood. "She must have been pushed."

"That has yet to be determined."

"I'm sure it has. I can't help you as to who she was, Lieutenant. As I don't have a twin, I can only—" She broke off, her color draining a second time. Now her free hand fisted and pressed hard to her stomach. "Oh, no. Oh, God."

He understood, didn't hesitate. "Who was she?"

"I— It could have been… She's stayed here before while I was away. That's why I stopped leaving a spare key outside. She might have had it copied, though. She'd think nothing of that."

Turning her gaze away from the outline, she walked back through the debris, sat on the arm of the sofa. "A cousin." Grace sipped brandy again, slowly, letting it ease warmth back into her system. "Melissa Bennington— No, I think she took the Fontaine back a few months ago, after the divorce. I'm not sure." She pushed a hand through her hair. "I wasn't interested enough to be sure of a detail like that."

"She resembles you?"

She offered a weak, humorless smile. "It's Melissa's mission to *be* me. I went from finding it mildly flattering to mildly annoying. In the last few years I found it pathetic. There's a surface resemblance, I suppose. She's augmented it. She let her hair grow, dyed it my color. There was some difference in build, but she… augmented that, as well. She shops the same stores, uses the same salons. Chooses the same men. We grew up together, more or less. She always felt I got the better deal on all manner of levels."

She made herself look back, look down, and felt a wash of grief and pity. "Apparently I did, this time around."

"If someone didn't know you well, could they mistake you?"

"A passing glance, I suppose. Maybe a casual acquaintance. No one who—" She broke off again, got to her feet. "You think someone killed her believing her to be me? Mistaking her for me, as you did? That's absurd. It was a break-in, a burglary. A terrible accident."

"It's possible." He had indeed taken out his book to note down her cousin's name. Now he glanced up, met her eyes. "It's also more than possible that someone came here, mistook her for you, and assumed she had the third Star."

She was good, he decided. There was barely a flicker in her eyes before she lied. "I have no idea what you're talking about."

"Yes, you do. And if you haven't been home since Wednesday, you still have it." He glanced down at the bag she continued to hold.

"I don't generally carry stars in my purse." She sent him a smile that was shaky around the edges. "But it's a lovely, almost poetic, thought. Now, I'm very tired—"

"Ms. Fontaine." His voice was clipped and cool. "This victim is the sixth body I've dealt with today that traces back to those three blue diamonds."

Her hand shot out, gripped his arm. "M.J. and Bailey?"

"Your friends are fine." He felt her grip go limp. "They've had an eventful holiday weekend, all of which could have been avoided if they'd contacted and cooperated with the police. And it's cooperation I'll have from you now, one way or the other."

She tossed her hair back. "Where are they? What did you do, toss them in a cell? My lawyer will have them out and your butt in a sling before you can finish reciting the Miranda." She started toward the phone, saw it wasn't on the Queen Anne table.

"No, they're not in a cell." It goaded him, the way she snapped into gear, ready to buck the rules. "I imagine they're planning your funeral right about now."

"Planning my—" Her fabulous eyes went huge with distress. "Oh, my God, you told them I was dead? They think I'm dead? Where are they? Where's the damn phone? I have to call them."

She crouched to push through the rubble, shoving at him when he took her arm again. "They're not home, either of them."

"You said they weren't in jail."

"And they're not." He could see he'd get nothing out of her until she'd satisfied herself. "I'll take you to them. Then we're going to sort this out, Ms. Fontaine—I promise you."

Grace didn't speak as he drove her toward the tidy suburbs edging D.C. He'd assured her that Bailey and M.J. were fine, and her instincts told her that Lieutenant Seth Buchanan was saying nothing but the truth.

Facts were his business, after all, she thought. But she still gripped her hands together until her knuckles ached.

She had to see them, touch them.

Guilt was already weighing on her, guilt that they should be grieving for her, when she'd spent the past few days indulging her need to be alone, to be away. To be somewhere else.

What had happened to them over the long weekend? Had they tried to contact her while she was out of reach? It was painfully obvious that the three blue diamonds Bailey had been assessing for the museum were at the bottom of it all.

As the afterimage of that stark outline on the chestnut floor flashed into her head, Grace shuddered once again.

Melissa. Poor, pathetic Melissa. But she couldn't think of that now. She couldn't think of anything but her friends.

"They're not hurt?" she managed to ask.

"No." Seth left it at that, drove through the wash of streetlights and headlights. Her scent was sliding silkily through his car, teasing his senses. Deliberately he opened his window and let the light, damp breeze chase it away. "Where have you been the last few days, Ms. Fontaine?"

"Away." Weary she laid her head back, shut her eyes. "It's one of my favorite spots."

She jerked upright again when he turned down a tree-lined street, then swung into the drive of a brick house. She saw a shiny Jaguar, then an impossibly decrepit boat of a car. But no spiffy MG, no practical little compact.

"Their cars aren't here," she began, tossing him a look of distrust and accusation.

"But they are."

She climbed out and, ignoring him, hurried toward the front door. Her knock was brisk, businesslike, but her fist trembled. The door opened, and a man she'd never seen before stared down at her. His cool green eyes flickered with shock, then slowly warmed. His flash of a smile was blinding. Then he reached out, laid a hand gently on her cheek.

"You're Grace."

"Yes, I—"

"It's absolutely wonderful to see you." He gathered her into his arms, one of which was freshly bandaged, with such easy affection that she didn't have time to register surprise. "I'm Cade," he murmured, his gaze meeting Seth's over Grace's head. "Cade Parris. Come on in."

"Bailey. M.J."

"Just in here. They'll be fine as soon as they see

you." He took her arm, felt the quick, hard tremors in it. But in the doorway of the living room, she stopped, laid a hand over his arm.

Inside, Bailey and M.J. stood, facing away, hands linked. Their voices were low, with tears wrenching through them. A man stood a short distance away, his hands thrust in his pockets and a look of helplessness on his bruised and battered face. When he saw her, his eyes, the gray of storm clouds, narrowed, flashed. Then smiled.

Grace took one shuddering breath, exhaled it slowly. "Well," she said in a clear, steady voice, "it's gratifying to know someone would weep copiously over me."

Both women whirled. For a moment, all three stared, three pair of eyes brimming over. To Seth's mind, they all moved as one, as a unit, so that their leaping rush across the room to each other held an uncanny and undeniably feminine grace. Then they were fused together, voices and tears mixing.

A triangle, he thought, frowning. With three points that made a whole. Like the golden triangle that held three priceless and powerful stones.

"I think they could use a little time," Cade said quietly, and gestured to the other man. "Lieutenant?" He motioned down the hall, lifting his brows when Seth hesitated. "I don't think they're going anywhere just now."

With a barely perceptible shrug, Seth stepped back. He could give them twenty minutes. "I need your phone."

"There's one in the kitchen. Want a beer, Jack?"

The third man grinned. "You're playing my song."

"Amnesia," Grace said a little time later. She and Bailey were huddled together on the sofa, with M.J. sitting on the floor at their feet. "Everything just blanked?"

"Everything." Bailey kept her hold on Grace's hand tight, afraid to break the link. "I woke up in this horrible little hotel room with no memory, over a million in cash, and the diamond. I picked Cade's name out of the phone book. Parris." She smiled a little. "Funny, isn't it?"

"I'm going to get you to France yet," Grace promised.

"He helped me through everything." The warmth in her tone had Grace sharing a quick look with M.J. This was something to be discussed in detail later. "I started to remember, piece by piece. You and M.J., just flashes. I could see your faces, even hear your voices, but nothing fit. He's the one who narrowed it down to Salvini, and when he took me there... He broke in."

"Shortly before we did," M.J. added. "Jack could tell the rear locks had been picked."

"We got inside," Bailey continued, and her tear-ravaged eyes went glassy. "And I remembered, I remembered it all then, how Thomas and Timothy were planning to steal the stones, copy them. How I'd shipped one off to each of you to keep it from happening. Stupid, so stupid."

"No, it wasn't." Grace slid an arm around Bailey's shoulders. "It makes perfect sense to me. You didn't have time for anything else."

"I should have called the police, but I was so sure I could turn things around. I was going into Thomas's office to have a showdown, tell them it was over. And I saw…" She trembled again. "The fight. Horrible. The lightning flashing through the windows, their faces. Then Timothy grabbed the letter opener, the knife. The power went out, but the lightning kept flashing, and I could see what he was doing…to Thomas. All the blood."

"Don't," M.J. murmured, rubbing a comforting hand on Bailey's knee. "Don't go back there."

"No." Bailey shook her head. "I have to. He saw me, Grace. He would have killed me. He came after me. I had grabbed the bag with their deposit money, and I ran through the dark. And I hid down under the stairs. In this little cave under the stairs. But I could see him hunting for me, blood all over his hands. I still don't remember how I got out, got to that room."

Grace couldn't bear to imagine it—her quiet, serious-minded friend, pursued by a murderer. "The important thing is that you did get away, and you're safe." Grace looked down at M.J. "We all are." She tried a bolstering grin. "And how did you spend your holiday?"

"On the run with a bounty hunter, handcuffed to a bed in a cheap motel, being shot at by a couple of creeps—with a little detour up to your place in the mountains."

Bounty hunter, Grace thought, trying to keep pace. The man named Jack, she supposed, with the bronze-tipped ponytail and the stormy gray eyes. And the killer grin. Handcuffs, cheap motels, and shootings. Pressing fingertips to her eyes, she latched on to the least disturbing detail.

"You were at my place? When?"

"It's a long story." M.J. gave a quick version of a handful of days from her first encounter with Jack, when he'd tried to take her in, believing her to be a bail jumper, to the two of them escaping that setup and working their way back to the core of the puzzle.

"We know someone's pulling the strings," M.J. concluded. "But we haven't gotten very far on figuring that out yet. The bail bondsman-cum-blackmailer who gave Jack the fake paperwork on me is dead, the two guys who came after us are dead, the Salvinis are dead."

"And Melissa," Grace murmured.

"It was Melissa?" Bailey turned to Grace. "In your house?"

"It must have been. When I got home, the cop was there. The place was torn up, and they'd assumed it was me." It took a moment, a carefully indrawn breath, a steady exhale, before she could finish. "She'd fallen off the balcony—or been pushed. I was miles away when it happened."

"Where did you go?" M.J. asked her. "When Jack and I got to your country place, it was locked up tight. I thought… I was sure you'd just been there. I could smell you."

"I left late yesterday morning. Got an itch to be near the water, so I drove down the Eastern Shore, found a little B-and-B. I did some antiquing, rubbed elbows with tourists, watched a fireworks display. I didn't leave until late today. I nearly stayed over another night. But I called both of you from the B-and-B and got your machines. I started feeling uncomfortable about being out of contact, so I headed home."

She shut her eyes a moment. "Bailey, I hadn't been really thinking. Just before I left for the country, we lost one of the children."

"Oh, Grace, I'm sorry."

"It happens all the time. They're born with AIDS or a crack addiction or a hole in the heart. Some of them die. But I can't get used to it, and it was on my mind.

So I wasn't really thinking. When I started back, I started to think. And I started to worry. Then the cop was there in my house. He asked about the stone. I didn't know what you wanted me to tell him."

"We've told the police everything now." Bailey sighed. "Neither Cade nor Jack seem to like this Buchanan very much, but they respect his abilities. The two stones are safe now, as we are."

"I'm sorry for what you went through, both of you. I'm sorry I wasn't here."

"It wouldn't have made any difference," M.J. declared. "We were scattered all over—one stone apiece. Maybe we were meant to be."

"Now we're together." Grace took each of their hands in hers. "What happens next?"

"Ladies." Seth stepped into the room, skimmed his cool gaze over them, then focused on Grace. "Ms. Fontaine. The diamond?"

She rose, picked up the purse she'd tossed carelessly on the end of the couch. Opening it, she took out a velvet pouch, slid the stone out into her palm. "Magnificent, isn't it?" she murmured, studying the flash of bold blue light. "Diamonds are supposed to be cold to the touch, aren't they, Bailey? Yet this has…heat." She lifted her eyes to Seth's as she crossed to him. "Still, how many lives is it worth?"

She held her open palm out. When his fingers closed

around the stone, she felt the jolt—his fingers on her skin, the shimmering blue diamond between their hands.

Something clicked, almost audibly.

She wondered if he'd felt it, heard it. Why else did those enigmatic eyes narrow, or his hand linger? The breath caught in her throat.

"Impressive, isn't it?" she managed, then felt the odd wave of emotion and recognition ebb when he took the stone from her hand.

He didn't care for the shock that had run up his arm, and he spoke bitingly. "I imagine this one's out of even your price range, Ms. Fontaine."

She merely smiled. No, she told herself, he couldn't have felt anything—and neither had she. Just imagination and stress. "I prefer to decorate my body in something less…obvious."

Bailey rose. "The Stars are my responsibility, unless and until the Smithsonian indicates otherwise." She looked over at Cade, who remained in the doorway. "We'll put them in the safe. All of them. And I'll speak with Dr. Linstrum in the morning."

Seth turned the stone over in his hand. He imagined he could confiscate it, and its mates. They were, after all, evidence in several homicides. But he didn't relish driving back to the station with a large fortune in his car.

Parris was an irritant, he reflected. But he was an honest one. And, technically, the stones were in Bailey James's keeping until the Smithsonian relieved her of them. He wondered just what the powers at the museum would have to say about the recent travels of the Three Stars.

But that wasn't his problem.

"Lock it up," he said, passing the stone off to Cade. "And I'll be talking with Dr. Linstrum in the morning, as well, Ms. James."

Cade took one quick, threatening step forward. "Look, Buchanan—"

"No." Quietly, Bailey stepped between them, a cool breeze between two building storms. "Lieutenant Buchanan's right, Cade. It's his business now."

"That doesn't stop it from being mine." He gave Seth one last, warning look. "Watch your step," he said, then walked away with the stone.

"Thank you for bringing Grace by so quickly, Lieutenant."

Seth looked down at the extended, and obviously dismissing, hand Bailey offered him. Here's your hat, he thought, what's your hurry. "I'm sorry you were disturbed, Ms. James." His gaze flicked over to M.J. "Ms. O'Leary. You'll keep available."

"We're not going anywhere." M.J.'s chin angled, a

cocky gesture as Jack crossed to her. "Drive carefully, Lieutenant."

He acknowledged the second dismissal with a slight nod. "Ms. Fontaine? I'll drive you back."

"She's not leaving." M.J. jumped in front of Grace like a tiger defending her cub. "She's not going back to that house tonight. She's staying here, with us."

"You may not care to go back home, Ms. Fontaine," Seth said coolly. "You may find it more comfortable to answer questions in my office."

"You can't be serious—"

He cut Bailey's protest off with a look. "I have a body in the morgue. I take it very seriously."

"You're a class act, Buchanan," Jack drawled, but the sound was low and threatening. "Why don't you and I go in the other room and...talk about our options?"

"It's all right." Grace stepped forward, working up a believable smile. "It's Jack, isn't it?"

"That's right." He took his attention from Buchanan long enough to smile at her. "Jack Dakota. Pleased to meet you... Miss April."

"Oh, my misspent youth survives." With a little laugh, she kissed his bruised cheek. "I appreciate the offer to beat up the lieutenant for me, Jack, but you look like you've already gone several rounds."

Grinning now, he stroked a thumb over his bruised jaw. "I've got a few more rounds in me."

"I don't doubt it. But, sad to say, the cop's right." She pushed her hair to her back and turned that smile, several degrees cooler now, on Seth. "Tactless, but right. He needs some answers. I need to go back."

"You're not going back to your house alone," Bailey insisted. "Not tonight, Grace."

"I'll be fine. But if it's all right with your Cade, I'll deal with this, pick up a few things and come back." She glanced over at Cade as he came back into the room. "Got a spare bed, darling?"

"You bet. Why don't I go with you, help you pick up your things and bring you back?"

"You stay here with Bailey." She kissed him, as well—a casual and already affectionate brush of lips. "I'm sure Lieutenant Buchanan and I will manage." She picked up her purse, turned and embraced both M.J. and Bailey again. "Don't worry about me. After all, I'm in the arms of the law."

She eased back, shot Seth one of those full candle-power smiles. "Isn't that right, Lieutenant?"

"In a manner of speaking." He stepped back and waited for her to walk to the door ahead of him.

She waited until they were in his car and pulling out of the drive. "I need to see the body." She didn't look at him, but lifted a hand to the four people crowded at the front door, watching them drive away. "You need— She'll have to be identified, won't she?"

It surprised him that she'd take the duty on. "Yes."

"Then let's get it over with. After—afterwards, I'll answer your questions. I'd prefer we handle that in your office," she added, using that smile again. "My house isn't ready for company."

"Fine."

She'd known it would be hard. She'd known it would be horrible. Grace had prepared herself for it—or she'd thought she had. Nothing, she realized as she stared down at what remained of the woman in the morgue, could have prepared her.

It was hardly surprising that they'd mistaken Melissa for her. The face Melissa had been so proud of was utterly ruined. Death had been cruel here, and, through her involvement with the hospital, Grace had reason to know it often was.

"It's Melissa." Her voice echoed flatly in the chilly white room. "My cousin, Melissa Fontaine."

"You're sure?"

"Yes. We shared the same health club, among other things. I know her body as well as I know mine. She has a sickle-shaped birthmark at the small of her back, just left of center. And there's a scar on the bottom of her left foot, small, crescent-shaped, in the ball of her foot, where she stepped on a broken shell in the Hamptons when we were twelve."

Seth shifted, found the scar, then nodded to the M.E.'s assistant. "I'm sorry for your loss."

"Yes, I'm sure you are." With muscles that felt like glass, she turned, her dimming vision passing over him. "Excuse me."

She made it nearly to the door before she swayed. Swearing under his breath, Seth caught her, pulled her out into the corridor and put her in a chair. With one hand, he shoved her head between her knees.

"I'm not going to faint." She squeezed her eyes tightly shut, battling fiercely against the twin foes of dizziness and nausea.

"Could have fooled me."

"I'm much too sophisticated for something as maudlin as a swoon." But her voice broke, her shoulders sagged, and for a moment she kept her head down. "Oh, God, she's dead. And all because she hated me."

"What?"

"Doesn't matter. She's dead." Bracing herself, she sat up again, let her head rest against the cold white wall. Her cheeks were just as colorless. "I have to call my aunt. Her mother. I have to tell her what happened."

He gauged this woman, studying the face that was no less staggeringly lovely for being bone-white. "Give me the name. I'll take care of it."

"It's Helen Wilson Fontaine. I'll do it."

He didn't realize until her hand moved that he'd

placed his own over it. He pulled back on every level, and rose. "I haven't been able to reach Helen Fontaine or her husband. She's in Europe."

"I know where she is." Grace shook back her hair, but didn't try to stand. Not yet. "I can find her." The thought of making that call, saying what had to be said, squeezed her throat. "Could I have some water, Lieutenant?"

His heels echoed on tile as he strode off. Then there was silence—a full, damning silence that whispered of what kind of business was done in such places. There were scents here that slid slyly under the potent odors of antiseptics and industrial cleaning solutions.

She was pitifully grateful when she heard his footsteps on the return journey.

She took the paper cup from him with both hands, drinking slowly, concentrating on the simple act of swallowing liquid.

"Why did she hate you?"

"What?"

"Your cousin. You said she hated you. Why?"

"Family trait," she said briefly. She handed him back the empty cup as she rose. "I'd like to go now."

He took her measure a second time. Her color had yet to return, her pupils were dilated, the electric-blue irises were glassy. He doubted she'd last another hour.

"I'll take you back to Parris's," he decided. "You can

get your things in the morning, come in to my office to make your statement."

"I said I'd do it tonight."

"And I say you'll do it in the morning. You're no good to me now."

She tried a weak laugh. "Why, Lieutenant, I believe you're the first man who's ever said that to me. I'm crushed."

"Don't waste the routine on me." He took her arm, led her to the outside doors. "You haven't got the energy for it."

He was exactly right. She pulled her arm free as they stepped back into the thick night air. "I don't like you."

"You don't have to." He opened the car door, waited. "Any more than I have to like you."

She stepped to the door, and with it between them met his eyes. "But the difference is, if I had the energy—or the inclination—I could make you sit up and beg."

She got in, sliding those long, silky legs in.

Not likely, Seth told himself as he shut the door with a snap. But he wasn't entirely sure he believed it.

Chapter 3

She felt like a weakling, but she didn't go home. She'd needed friends, not that empty house, with the shadow of a body drawn on the floor.

Jack had gone over, fetched her bags out of her car and brought them to her. For a day, at least, she was content to make do with that.

Since she was driving in to meet with Seth, Grace had made do carefully. She'd dressed in a summer suit she'd just picked up on the Shore. The little short skirt and waist-length jacket in buttercup yellow weren't precisely professional—but she wasn't aiming for professional. She'd taken the time to catch her waterfall of hair back in a complicated French braid and made up her face with the concentration and determination of a general plotting a decisive battle.

Meeting with Seth again felt like a battle.

Her stomach was still raw from the call she'd made to her aunt, and the sickness that had overwhelmed her after it. She'd slept poorly, but she had slept, tucked into one of Cade's guest rooms, secure that those who meant most to her were close by.

She would deal with the relatives later, she thought, easing her convertible into the lot at the station house. It would be hard, but she would deal with them. For now, she had to deal with herself. And Seth Buchanan.

If anyone had been watching as she stepped from her car and started across the lot, he would have seen a transformation. Subtly, gradually, her eyes went from weary to sultry. Her gait loosened, eased into a lazy, hip-swinging walk designed to cross a man's eyes. Her mouth turned up slightly at the corners, into a secret, knowing female smile.

It wasn't really a mask, but another part of her. Innate and habitual, it was an image she could draw on at will. She willed it now, flashing a slow under-the-lashes smile at the uniform who stepped to the door as she did. He flushed, moved back and nearly bobbled the door in his hurry to open it for her.

"Why, thank you, Officer."

Heat rose up his neck, into his face, and made her smile widen. She was right on target. Seth Buchanan wouldn't see a pale, trembling woman this morning. He'd see Grace Fontaine, just hitting her stride.

She sauntered up to the sergeant on duty at the desk, skimmed a fingertip along the edge. "Excuse me?"

"Yes, ma'am." His Adam's apple bobbed three times as he swallowed.

"I wonder if you could help me? I'm looking for a Lieutenant Buchanan. Are you in charge?" She skimmed her gaze over him. "You must be in charge, Commander."

"Ah, yes. No. It's sergeant." He fumbled for the sign-in book, the passes. "I— He's— You'll find the lieutenant upstairs, detective division. To the left of the stairs."

"Oh." She took the pen he offered and signed her name boldly. "Thank you, Commander. I mean, Sergeant."

She heard his little expulsion of breath as she turned, and felt his gaze on her legs as she climbed the stairs.

She found the detective division easily enough. One sweeping glance took in the front-to-front desks, some manned, some not. The cops were in shirtsleeves in an oppressive heat that was barely touched by what had to be a faulty air-conditioning unit. A lot of guns, she thought, a lot of half-eaten meals and empty cups of coffee. Phones shrilling.

She picked her mark—a man with a loosened tie, feet on the desk, a report of some kind in one hand

and a Danish in the other. As she started through the crowded room, several conversations stopped. Someone whistled softly—it was like a sigh. The man at the desk swept his feet to the floor, swallowed the Danish.

"Ma'am."

About thirty, she judged, though his hairline was receding rapidly. He wiped his crumb-dusted fingers on his shirt, rolled his eyes slightly to the left, where one of his associates was grinning and pounding a fist to his heart.

"I hope you can help me." She kept her eyes on his, and only his, until a muscle began to twitch in his jaw. "Detective?"

"Yeah, ah, Carter, Detective Carter. What can I do for you?"

"I hope I'm in the right place." For effect, she turned her head, swept her gaze over the room and its occupants. Several stomachs were ruthlessly sucked in. "I'm looking for Lieutenant Buchanan. I think he's expecting me." Gracefully she brushed a loose flutter of hair away from her face. "I'm afraid I just don't know the proper procedure."

"He's in his office. Back in his office." Without taking his eyes from her he jerked a thumb. "Belinski, tell the lieutenant he has a visitor. A Miss…"

"It's Grace." She slid a hip onto the corner of the desk, letting her skirt hike up a dangerous inch. "Grace

Fontaine. Is it all right if I wait here, Detective Carter? Am I interrupting your work?"

"Yes— No. Sure."

"It's so exciting." She brought the temperature of the overheated room up ten more degrees with a dazzling smile. "Detective work. You must have so many interesting stories."

By the time Seth had finished the phone call he was on when he was notified of Grace's arrival, shrugged back into the jacket he'd removed as a concession to the heat and made his way into the bull pen, Carter's desk was completely surrounded. He heard a low, throaty female laugh rise out of the center of the crowd.

And saw a half a dozen of his best men panting like puppies over a meaty bone.

The woman, he decided, was going to be an enormous headache.

"I see all cases have been closed this morning, and miraculously crime has come to a halt."

His voice had the desired effect. Several men jerked straight. Those less easily intimidated grinned as they skulked back to their desks. Deserted, Carter flushed from his neck to his receding sandy hairline. "Ah, Grace—that is, Miss Fontaine to see you, Lieutenant. Sir."

"So I see. You finish that report, Detective?"

"Working on it." Carter grabbed the papers he'd tossed aside and buried his nose in them.

"Ms. Fontaine." Seth arched a brow, gestured toward his office.

"It was nice meeting you, Michael." Grace trailed a finger over Carter's shoulder as she passed.

He'd feel the heat of that skimming touch for hours.

"You can cut the power back now," Seth said dryly as he opened the door to his office. "You won't need it."

"You never know, do you?" She sauntered in, moving past him, close enough for them to brush bodies. She thought she felt him stiffen, just a little, but his eyes remained level, cool, and apparently unimpressed. Miffed, she studied his office.

The institutional beige of the walls blended depressingly into the dingy beige of the aging linoleum floor. An overburdened department-issue desk, gray file cabinets, computer, phone and one small window didn't add any spark to the no-nonsense room.

"So this is where the mighty rule," she murmured. It disappointed her that she found no personal touches. No photos, no sports trophies. Nothing she could hold on to, no sign of the man behind the badge.

As she had in the bull pen, she eased a hip onto the corner of his desk. To say she resembled a sunbeam would have been a cliché. And it would have been incorrect, Seth decided. Sunbeams were tame—warm, welcoming. She was an explosive bolt of heat lightning— Hot. Fatal.

A blind man would have noticed those satiny legs in the snug yellow skirt. Seth merely walked around, sat, looked at her face.

"You'd be more comfortable in a chair."

"I'm fine here." Idly she picked up a pen, twirled it. "I don't suppose this is where you interrogate suspects."

"No, we have a dungeon downstairs for that."

Under other circumstances, she would have appreciated his dust-dry tone. "Am I a suspect?"

"I'll let you know." He angled his head. "You recover quickly, Ms. Fontaine."

"Yes, I do. You had questions, Lieutenant?"

"Yes, I do. Sit down. In a chair."

Her lips moved in what was nearly a pout. A luscious come-on-and-kiss-me pout. He felt the quick, helpless pull of lust, and damned her for it. She moved, sliding off the desk, settling into a chair, taking her time crossing those killer legs.

"Better?"

"Where were you Saturday, between the hours of midnight and 3:00 a.m.?"

So that was when it had happened, she thought, and ignored the ache in her stomach. "Aren't you going to read me my rights?"

"You're not charged, you don't need a lawyer. It's a simple question."

"I was in the country. I have a house in western Maryland. I was alone. I don't have an alibi. Do I need a lawyer now?"

"Do you want to complicate this, Ms. Fontaine?"

"There's no way to simplify it, is there?" But she flicked a hand in dismissal. The thin diamond bracelet that circled her wrist shot fire. "All right, Lieutenant, as uncomplicated as possible. I don't want my lawyer—for the moment. Why don't I just give you a basic rundown? I left for the country on Wednesday. I wasn't expecting my cousin, or anyone, for that matter. I did have contact with a few people over the weekend. I bought a few supplies in the town nearby, shopped at the gardening stand. That would have been Friday afternoon. I picked up some mail on Saturday. It's a small town, the postmistress would remember. That was before noon, however, which would give me plenty of time to drive back. And, of course, there was the courier who delivered Bailey's package on Friday."

"And you didn't find that odd? Your friend sends you a blue diamond, and you just shrug it off and go shopping?"

"I called her. She wasn't in." She arched a brow. "But you probably know that. I did find it odd, but I had things on my mind."

"Such as?"

Her lips curved, but the smile wasn't reflected in her eyes. "I'm not required to tell you my thoughts. I did wonder about it and worried a little. I thought perhaps it was a copy, but I didn't really believe that. A copy couldn't have what that stone has. Bailey's instructions in the package were to keep it with me until she contacted me. So that's what I did."

"No questions?"

"I rarely question people I trust."

He tapped a pencil on the edge of the desk. "You stayed alone in the country until Monday, when you drove back to the city."

"No. I drove down to the Eastern Shore on Sunday. I had a whim." She smiled again. "I often do. I stayed at a bed-and-breakfast."

"You didn't like your cousin?"

"No, I didn't." She imagined that quick shift of topic was an interrogation technique. "She was difficult to like, and I rarely make the effort with difficult people. We were raised together after my parents were killed, but we weren't close. I intruded into her life, into her space. She compensated for it by being disagreeable. I was often disagreeable in return. As we got older, she had a less…successful talent with men than I. Apparently she thought by enhancing the similarities in our appearance, she'd have better success."

"And did she?"

"I suppose it depends on your point of view. Melissa enjoyed men." To combat the guilt coating her heart, Grace leaned back negligently in the chair. "She certainly enjoyed men—which is one of the reasons she was recently divorced. She preferred the species in quantity."

"And how did her husband feel about that?"

"Bobbie's a…" She trailed off, then relieved a great deal of her own tension with a quick, delighted and very appealing laugh. "If you're suggesting that Bobbie—her ex—tracked her down to my house, murdered her, trashed the place and walked off whistling, you couldn't be more wrong. He's a cream puff. And he is, I believe, in England, even as we speak. He enjoys tennis and never misses Wimbledon. You can check easily enough."

Which he would, Seth thought, noting it down. "Some people find murder distasteful on a personal level, but not at a distance. They just pay for a service."

This time she sighed. "We both know Melissa wasn't the target, Lieutenant. I was. She was in my house." Restless, she rose, a graceful and feline movement. Walking to the tiny window, she looked out on his dismal view. "She's made herself at home in my Potomac house twice before when I was away. The first time, I tolerated it. The second, she enjoyed the facilities a bit too enthusiastically for my taste. We had a spat about it. She left in a huff, and I removed the spare key. I should have thought to change the locks, but it never occurred to me she'd go to the trouble of having copies made."

"When was the last time you saw her or spoke with her?"

Grace sighed. Dates ran through her head, people, events, meaningless social forays. "About six weeks ago, maybe eight. At the health club. We ran into each other in the steam room, didn't have much conversation. We never had much to say to each other."

She was regretting that now, Seth realized. Going over in her head opportunities lost or wasted. And it would do no good. "Would she have opened the door to someone she didn't know?"

"If the someone was male and was marginally attractive, yes." Weary of the interview, she turned back. "Look, I don't know what else I can tell you, what help I can possibly be. She was a careless, often arrogant woman. She picked up strange men in bars when she felt the urge. She let someone in that night, and she died for it. Whatever she was, she didn't deserve to die for that."

She brushed at her hair absently, tried to clear her mind as Seth simply sat, waiting. "Maybe he demanded she give him the stone. She wouldn't have understood. She paid for her trespassing, for her carelessness and her ignorance. And the stone is back with Bailey, where it belongs. If you haven't spoken to Dr. Linstrum yet this morning, I can tell you that Bailey should be meeting with him right now. I don't know anything else to tell you."

He kicked back for a moment, his eyes cool and steady on her face. If he discounted the connection with the diamonds, it could play another way. Two women, at odds all their lives. One of them returns home unexpectedly to find the other in her home. An argument. Escalating into a fight. And one of them ends up taking a dive off a second-floor balcony into a pool of glass.

The first woman doesn't panic. She trashes her own home to cover herself, then drives away. Puts distance between herself and the scene.

Was she a skilled enough actress to fake that stark shock, the raw emotion he'd seen on her face the night before?

He thought she was.

But despite that, the scene just didn't click. There was the undeniable connection of the diamonds. And he was dead sure that if Grace Fontaine had caused her cousin's fall, she would have been just as capable of picking up the phone and coolly reporting an accident.

"All right, that's all for now."

"Well." Her breath was a huff of relief. "That wasn't so bad, all in all."

He stood up. "I'll have to ask you to stay available."

She switched on the charm again, a hot, rose-colored light. "I'm always available, handsome. Ask anyone." She picked up her purse, moved with him to the door. "How long before I can have my house dealt with? I'd like to put things back to order as quickly as possible."

"I'll let you know." He glanced at his watch. "When you're up to going through things and doing an inventory to see what's missing, I'd like you to contact me."

"I'm on my way over now to do just that."

His brow furrowed a moment as he juggled responsibilities. He could assign a man to go with her, but he preferred dealing with it himself. "I'll follow you over."

"Police protection?"

"If necessary."

"I'm touched. Why don't I give you a lift, handsome?"

"I'll follow you over," he repeated.

"Suit yourself," she began, and grazed a hand over his cheek. Her eyes widened slightly as his fingers clamped on her wrist. "Don't like to be petted?" She purred the words, surprised at how her heart had jumped and started to race. "Most animals do."

His face was very close to hers, their bodies were just touching, with the heat from the room and something even more sweltering between them. Something old, and almost familiar.

He drew her hand down slowly, kept his fingers on her wrist.

"Be careful what buttons you push."

Excitement, she realized with surprise. It was pure, primal excitement that zipped through her. "Wasted advice," she said silkily, daring him. "I enjoy pushing new ones. And apparently you have a few interesting buttons just begging for attention." She skimmed her gaze deliberately down to his mouth. "Just begging."

He could imagine himself shoving her back against the door, moving fast into that heat, feeling her go molten. Because he was certain she was aware of just how perfectly a man would imagine it, he stepped back, released her and opened the door to the din of the bull pen.

"Be sure to turn in your visitor's badge at the desk," he said.

He was a cool one, Grace thought as she drove. An attractive, successful, unmarried—she'd slipped that bit of data out of an unsuspecting Detective Carter— and self-contained man.

A challenge.

And, she decided as she passed through the quiet, well-designed neighborhood, toward her home, a challenge was exactly what she needed to get through the emotional upheaval.

She'd have to face her aunt in a few hours, and the rest of the relatives soon after. There would be questions, demands, and, she knew, blame. She would be the recipient of all of it. That was the way her family worked, and that was what she'd come to expect from them.

Ask Grace, take from Grace, point the finger at Grace. She wondered how much of that she deserved, and how much had simply been inherited along with the money her parents left her.

It hardly mattered, she thought, since both were hers, like it or not.

She swung into her drive, her gaze sweeping over and up. The house was something she'd wanted. The clever and unique design of wood and glass, the gables, the cornices, the decks and the ruthlessly groomed grounds. She'd wanted the space, the elegance that lent itself to entertaining, the convenience to the city. The proximity to Bailey and M.J.

But the little house in the mountains was something she'd needed. And that was hers, and hers alone. The relatives didn't know it existed. No one could find her there unless she wanted to be found.

But here, she thought as she set the brakes, was the neat, expensive home of one Grace Fontaine. Heiress, socialite and party girl. The former centerfold, the Radcliffe graduate, the Washington hostess.

Could she continue to live here, she wondered, with death haunting the rooms? Time would tell.

For now, she was going to concentrate on solving the puzzle of Seth Buchanan, and finding a way under that seemingly impenetrable armor of his.

Just for the fun of it.

She heard him pull in and, in a deliberately provocative move, turned, tipped down her shaded glasses and studied him over the tops.

Oh, yes, she thought. He was very, very attractive. The way he controlled that lean and muscled body. Very economical. No wasted movements. He wouldn't waste them in bed, either. And she wondered just how long it would be before she could lure him there. She had a hunch—and she rarely doubted her hunches where men were concerned—that there was a volcano bubbling under that calm and somewhat austere surface.

She was going to enjoy poking at it until it erupted.

As he crossed to her, she handed him her keys. "Oh, but you have your own now, don't you?" She tipped her glasses back into place. "Well, use mine…this time."

"Who else has a set?"

She skimmed the tip of her tongue over her top lip, darkly pleased when she saw his gaze jerk down. Just for an instant, but it was progress. "Bailey and M.J. I don't give my keys to men. I'd rather open the door for them myself. Or close it."

"Fine." He dumped the keys back in her hand, looking amused when her brows drew together. "Open the door."

One step forward, two steps back, she mused, then stepped up on the flagstone portico and unlocked her home.

She'd braced for it, but it was still difficult. The foyer was as it had been, largely undisturbed. But her gaze was drawn up now, helplessly, to the shattered railing.

"It's a long way to fall," she murmured. "I wonder if you have time to think, to understand, on the way down."

"She wouldn't have."

"No." And that was better, somehow. "I suppose not." She stepped into the living area, forced herself to look at the chalk outline. "Well, where to begin?"

"He got to your safe down here. Emptied it. You'll want to list what was taken out."

"The library safe." She moved through, under an arch and into a wide room filled with light and books. A great many of those books littered the floor now, and an art deco lamp in the shape of an elongated woman's body—a small thing she'd loved—was cracked in two. "He wasn't subtle, was he?"

"I say he was rushed. And pissed off."

"You'd know best." She walked to the safe, noting the open door and the empty interior. "I had some jewelry—quite a bit, actually. A few thousand in cash."

"Bonds, stock certificates?"

"No, they're in my safe-deposit box at the bank. One doesn't need to take out stock certificates and enjoy the way they sparkle. I bought a terrific pair of diamond earrings just last month." She sighed, shrugged. "Gone now. I have a complete list of my jewelry, and photographs of each piece, along with the insurance papers, in my safety box. Replacing them's just a matter of—"

She broke off, made a small, distressed sound and rushed from the room,

The woman could move when she wanted, Seth thought as he headed upstairs after her. And she didn't lose any of that feline grace with speed. He turned into her bedroom, then into her walk-in closet behind her.

"He wouldn't have found it. He couldn't have found it." She repeated the words like a prayer as she twisted a knob on the built-in cabinet. It swung out, revealing a safe in the wall behind.

Quickly, her fingers not quite steady, she spun the combination, wrenched open the door. Her breath expelled in a whoosh as she knelt and took out velvet boxes and bags.

More jewelry, he thought with a shake of his head.

How many earrings could one woman wear? But she was opening each box carefully, examining the contents.

"These were my mother's," she murmured, with a catch of undiluted emotion in the words. "They matter. The sapphire pin my father gave her for their fifth anniversary, the necklace he gave her when I was born. The pearls. She wore these the day they married." She stroked the creamy white strand over her cheek as if it were a loved one's hand. "I had this built for them, didn't keep them with the others. Just in case."

She sat back on her heels, her lap filled with jewelry that meant so much more than gold and pretty stones. "Well," she managed as her throat closed. "Well, they're here. They're still here."

"Ms. Fontaine."

"Oh, call me Grace," she snapped. "You're as stuffy as my Uncle Niles." Then she pressed a hand to her forehead, trying to work away the beginnings of a tension headache. "I don't suppose you can make coffee."

"Yes, I can make coffee."

"Then why don't you go down and do that little thing, handsome, and give me a minute here?"

He surprised her, and himself, by crouching down first, laying a hand on her shoulder. "You could have lost the pearls, lost all of it. You still wouldn't have lost your memories."

Uneasy that he'd felt compelled to say it, he straightened and left her alone. He went directly to the kitchen, pushing through the mess to fill the coffeepot. He set it up to brew and switched the machine on. Stuck his hands in his pockets, then pulled them out.

What the hell was going on? he asked himself. He should be focused on the case, and the case alone. Instead, he felt himself being pulled, tugged at, by the woman upstairs—by the various faces of that woman. Bold, fragile, sexy, sensitive.

Just which was she? And why had he spent most of the night with her face lodged in his dreams?

He shouldn't even be here, he admitted. He had no official reason to be spending this time with her. It was true he felt the case warranted his personal attention. It was serious enough. But she was only one small part of the whole.

And he'd be lying to himself if he said he was here strictly on an investigation.

He found two undamaged cups. There were several broken ones lying around. Good Meissen china, he noted. His mother had a set she prized dearly. He was just pouring the coffee when he sensed her behind him.

"Black?"

"That's fine." She stepped in, and winced as she took a visual inventory of the kitchen. "He didn't miss much, did he? I suppose he thought I might stick a big blue diamond in my coffee canister or cookie jar."

"People put their valuables in a lot of odd places. I was involved in a burglary case once where the victim saved her in-house cash because she'd kept it in a sealed plastic bag in the bottom of the diaper pail. What self-respecting B-and-E man is going to paw through diapers?"

She chuckled, sipped her coffee. Whether or not it had been his purpose, his telling of the story had made her feel better. "It makes keeping things in a safe seem foolish. This one didn't take the silver, or any of the electronics. I suppose, as you said, he was in too much of a hurry, and just took what he could stuff in his pockets."

She walked to the kitchen window and looked out. "Melissa's clothes are upstairs. I didn't see her purse. He might have taken that, too, or it could just be buried under the mess."

"We'd have found it if it had been here."

She nodded. "I'd forgotten. You've already searched through my things." She turned back, leaned on the counter and eyed him over the rim of her cup. "Did you go through them personally, Lieutenant?"

He thought of the red silk gown. "Some of it. You have your own department store here."

"I'd come by that naturally, wouldn't I? I have a

weakness for things. All manner of things. You make excellent coffee, Lieutenant. Isn't there anyone who brews it for you in the morning?"

"No. Not at the moment." He set his coffee aside. "That wasn't very subtle."

"It wasn't intended to be. It's not that I mind competition. I just like to know if I have any. I still don't think I like you, but that could change." She lifted a hand to finger the tail of her braid. "Why not be prepared?"

"I'm interested in closing a case, not in playing games with you... Grace."

It was such a cool delivery, so utterly dispassionate it kindled her spirit of competition. "I suppose you don't like aggressive women."

"Not particularly."

"Well, then." She smiled as she stepped closer to him. "You're just going to hate this."

In a slick and practiced move, she slid a hand up into his hair and brought his mouth to hers.

Chapter 4

The jolt, lightning wrapped in black velvet, stabbed through him in one powerful strike. His head spun with it, his blood churned, his belly ached. No part of his system was spared the rapid onslaught of that lush and knowing mouth.

Her taste, unexpected yet familiar, plunged into him like hot spiced wine that rushed immediately to his head, leaving him dazed and drunk and desperate.

His muscles bunched, as if poised to leap. And in leaping, he would possess what was somehow already his. It took a vicious twist of will to keep his arms locked at his sides, when they strained to reach out, take, relish. Her scent was as dark, as drugging, as her flavor. Even the low, persuasive hum that sounded in her throat as she moved that glorious fantasy of a body against his was a tantalizing hint of what could be.

For a slow count of five, he fisted his hands, then relaxed them and let the internal war rage while his lips remained passive, his body rigid in denial.

He wouldn't give her the satisfaction of response....

She knew it was a mistake. Even as she moved toward him, reached for him, she'd known it. She'd made mistakes before, and she tried never to regret what was done and couldn't be undone.

But she regretted this.

She deeply regretted that his taste was utterly unique and perfect for her palate. That the texture of his hair, the shape of his shoulders, the strong wall of his chest, all taunted her, when she'd only meant to taunt him, to show him what she could offer. If she chose.

Instead, swept into need, rushed into it by that mating of lips, she offered more than she'd intended. And he gave nothing back.

She caught his bottom lip between her teeth, one quick, sharp nip, then masked an outrageous rush of disappointment by stepping casually back and aiming an amused smile at him.

"My, my, you're a cool one, aren't you, Lieutenant?"

His blood burned with every heartbeat, but he merely inclined his head. "You're not used to being resistible, are you, Grace?"

"No." She rubbed a fingertip lightly over her lip in a movement that was both absent and provocative. The essence of him clung stubbornly there, insisting it belonged. "But then, most of the men I've kissed haven't had ice water in their veins. It's a shame." She took her finger from her own lip, tapped it on his. "Such a nice mouth. Such potential. Still, maybe you just don't care for...women."

The grin he flashed stunned her. His eyes glowed with it, in fascinating tones of gold. His mouth softened with a charm that had a wicked and unpredictable appeal. Suddenly he was approachable, nearly boyish, and it made her heart yearn.

"Maybe," he said, "you're just not my type."

She gave one short, humorless laugh. "Darling, I'm every man's type. Well, we'll just chalk it up to a failed experiment and move on." Telling herself it was foolish to be hurt, she stepped to him again, reached up to straighten the tie she'd loosened.

He didn't want her to touch him, not then, not when he was so precariously perched on the edge. "You've got a hell of an ego there."

"I suppose I do." With her hands still on his tie, she looked up, into his eyes. The hell with it, she thought, if they couldn't be lovers, maybe they could be cautious friends. The man who had looked at her and grinned would be a good, solid friend.

So she smiled at him with a sweetness that was without art or guile, lancing his heart with one clean blow. "But then, men are generally predictable. You're just the exception to the rule, Seth, the one that proves it."

She brushed her hands down, smoothing his jacket and said something more, but he didn't hear it over the roaring in his ears. His control broke; he felt the snap, like the twang of a sword violently broken over an armored knee. In a movement he was hardly aware of, he spun her around, pressed her back against the wall, and was ravaging her mouth.

Her heart kicked in her chest, drove the breath out of her body. She gripped his shoulders as much for balance as in response to the sudden, violent need that shot from him to her and fused them together.

She yielded, utterly, then locked her arms around his neck and poured herself back.

Here, was all her dazzled mind could think. Oh, here, at last.

His hands raced over her, molded and somehow recognized each curve. And the recognition seared through him, as hot and real as the surge of desire. He wanted that taste, had to have it inside him, to swallow it whole. He assaulted her mouth like a man feeding after a lifelong fast, filled himself with the flavors of her, all of them dark, ripe, succulent.

She was there for him, had always been there—

impossibly there. And he knew that if he didn't pull back, he'd never be able to survive without her.

He slapped his hands on the wall on either side of her head to stop himself from touching, to stop himself from taking. Fighting to regain both his breath and his sanity, he eased out of the kiss, stepped away.

She continued to lean back against the wall, her eyes closed, her skin luminous with passion. By the time her lashes fluttered up and those slumberous blue eyes focused, he had his control snapped back ruthlessly in place.

"Unpredictable," she managed, barely resisting the urge to press both hands to her galloping heart. "Very."

"I warned you about pushing the wrong buttons." His voice was cool, edging toward cold, and had the effect of a backhand slap.

She flinched from it, might have reeled, if she hadn't been braced by the wall. His eyes narrowed fractionally at the reaction. Hurt? he wondered. No, that was ridiculous. She was a veteran game player and knew all the angles.

"Yes, you did." She straightened, pride stiffening her spine and forcing her lips to curve in a casual smile. "I'm just so resistant to warnings."

He thought she should be required by law to carry one—Danger! Woman!

"I've got work to do. I can give you another five

minutes, if you want me to wait while you pack some things."

Oh, you bastard, she thought. How can you be so cool, so unaffected? "You toddle right along, handsome. I'll be fine."

"I'd prefer you weren't in the house alone for the moment. Go pack some things."

"It's my home."

"Right now, it's a crime scene. You're down to four and a half minutes."

Fury vibrated through her in hot, pulsing beats. "I don't need anything here." She turned, started out, whirling back when he took her arm. "What?"

"You need clothes," he said, patient now. "For a day or two."

"Do you really think I'd wear anything that bastard might have touched?"

"That's a foolish and a predictable reaction." His tone didn't soften in the least. "You're not a foolish or a predictable woman. Don't be a victim, Grace. Go pack your things."

He was right. She could have despised him for that alone. But the frustrated need still fisted inside her was a much better reason. She said nothing at all, simply turned again and walked away.

When he didn't hear the front door slam, he was satisfied that she'd gone upstairs to pack, as he'd told her to. Seth turned off the coffeemaker, rinsed the cups and set them in the sink, then went out to wait for her.

She was a fascinating woman, he thought. Full of temperament, energy and ego. And she was undoing him, knot by carefully tied knot. How she knew exactly what strings to pull to do so was just one more mystery.

He'd taken this case on, he reminded himself. Riding a desk and delegating were only part of the job. He needed to be involved, and he'd involved himself with this—and therefore with her. Grace's part of the whole was small, but he needed to treat her with the same objectivity that he treated every other piece of the case with.

He looked up, his gaze drawn to the portrait that smiled down so invitingly.

He'd have to be more machine than man to stay objective when it came to Grace Fontaine.

It was midafternoon before he could clear his desk enough to handle a follow-up interview. The diamonds were the key, and he wanted another look at them. He hadn't been surprised when his phone conversation with Dr. Linstrum at the Smithsonian resulted in a testimonial to Bailey James's integrity and skill. The diamonds she'd gone to such lengths to protect remained at Salvini, and in her care.

When Seth pulled into the parking lot of the elegant corner building just outside D.C. that housed Salvini, he nodded to the uniformed cop guarding the main door. And felt a faint tug of sympathy. The heat was brutal.

"Lieutenant." Despite a soggy uniform, the officer snapped to attention.

"Ms. James inside?"

"Yes, sir. The store's closed to the public for the next week." He indicated the darkened showroom through the thick glass doors with a jerk of the head. "We have a guard posted at every entrance, and Ms. James is on the lower level. It's easier access through the rear, Lieutenant."

"Fine. When's your relief, Officer?"

"I've got another hour." The cop didn't wipe his brow, but he wanted to. Seth Buchanan had a reputation for being a stickler. "Four-hour rotations, as per your orders, sir."

"Bring a bottle of water with you next time." Well aware that the uniform sagged the minute his back was turned, Seth rounded the building. After a brief conversation with the duty guard at the rear, he pressed the buzzer beside the reinforced steel door. "Lieutenant Buchanan," he said when Bailey answered through the intercom. "I'd like a few minutes."

It took her some time to get to the door. Seth visualized her coming out of the workroom on the lower level, winding down the short corridor, passing the stairs where she'd hidden from a killer only days before.

He'd been through the building himself twice, top to bottom. He knew that not everyone could have survived what she'd been through in there.

The locks clicked, the door opened. "Lieutenant." She smiled at the guard, silently apologizing for his miserable duty. "Please come in."

She looked neat and tidy, Seth thought, with her trim blouse and slacks, her blond hair scooped back. Only the faint shadows under her eyes spoke of the strain she'd been under.

"I spoke with Dr. Linstrum," Seth began.

"Yes, I expect you did. I'm very grateful for his understanding."

"The stones are back where they started."

She smiled a little. "Well, they're back where they were a few days ago. Who knows if they'll ever see Rome again. Can I get you something cold to drink?" She gestured toward a soft-drink machine standing brightly against a dark wall.

"I'll buy." He plugged in coins. "I'd like to see the diamonds, and have a few words with you."

"All right." She pressed the button for her choice, and retrieved the can that clunked down the shoot. "They're in the vault." She continued to speak as she led the way. "I've arranged to have the security and alarm system beefed up. We've had cameras in the showroom for a number of years, but I'll have them installed at the doors, as well, and for the upper and lower levels. All areas."

"That's wise." He concluded that there was a practical streak of common sense beneath the fragile exterior. "You'll run the business now?"

She opened a door, hesitated. "Yes. My stepfather left it to the three of us, with my stepbrothers sharing eighty percent between them. In the event any of us died without heirs, the shares go to the survivors." She drew in a breath. "I survived."

"That's something to be grateful for, Bailey, not guilty about."

"Yes, that's what Cade says. But you see, I once had the illusion, at least, that they were family. Have a seat, I'll get the Stars."

He moved into the work area, glanced at the equipment, the long worktable. Intrigued, he stepped closer, examining the glitter of colored stones, the twists of gold. It was going to be a necklace, he realized, running a fingertip over the silky length of a closely linked chain. Something bold, almost pagan.

"I needed to get back to work," she said from behind him. "To do something...different, my own, I suppose, before I faced dealing with these again."

She set down a padded box that held the trio of diamonds.

"Your design?" he asked, gesturing to the piece on the worktable.

"Yes. I see the piece in my head. I can't draw worth a lick, but I can visualize. I wanted to make something for M.J. and for Grace to..." She sighed, sat on the high stool. "Well, let's say to celebrate survival."

"And this is the one for Grace."

"Yes." She smiled, pleased that he'd sensed it. "I see something more streamlined for M.J. But this is Grace." Carefully she set the unfinished work in a tray, slid the padded box containing the Three Stars between them. "They never lose their impact. Each time I see them, it stuns."

"How long before you're finished with them?"

"I'd just begun when—when I had to stop." She cleared her throat. "I've verified their authenticity. They are blue diamonds. Still, both the museum and the insurance carrier prefer more in-depth verification. I'll be running a number of other tests beyond what I've already started or completed. A metallurgist is testing the triangle, but that will be given to me for further study in a day or two. It shouldn't take more than a week altogether before the museum can take possession."

He lifted a stone from the bed, knew as soon as it

was in his hand that it was the one Grace had carried with her. He told himself that was impossible. His untrained eye couldn't tell one stone from either of its mates.

Yet he felt her on it. In it.

"Will it be hard to part with them?"

"I should say no, after the past few days. But yes, it will."

Grace's eyes were this color, Seth realized. Not sapphire, but the blue of the rare, powerful diamond.

"Worth killing for," he said quietly, looking at the stone in his hand. "Dying for." Then, annoyed with himself, he set the stone down again. "Your stepbrothers had a client."

"Yes, they spoke of a client, argued about him. Thomas wanted to take the money, the initial deposit, and run."

The money was being checked now, but there wasn't much hope of tracing its source.

"Timothy told Thomas he was a fool, that he'd never be able to run far or fast enough. That he—the client—would find him. He's not even human. Timothy said that, or something like it. They were both afraid, terribly afraid, and terribly desperate."

"Over their heads."

"Yes, I think very much over their heads."

"It would have to be a collector. No one could move

these stones for resale." He glanced at the gems sparkling in their trays like pretty stars. "You acquire, buy
and sell to collectors of gems."

"Yes—certainly not on a scale like the Three Stars,
but yes." She skimmed her fingers absently through
her hair. "A client might come to us with a stone, or
a request for one. We'd also acquire certain gems on
spec, with a particular client in mind."

"You have a client list, then? Names, preferences?"

"Yes, and we have records of what a client had
purchased, or sold." She gripped her hands together.
"Thomas would have kept it, in his office. Timothy
would have copies in his. I'll find them for you."

He touched her shoulder lightly before she could
slide from the stool. "I'll get them."

She let out a breath of relief. She had yet to be able
to face going upstairs, into the room where she'd seen
murder. "Thank you."

He took out his notebook. "If I asked you to name
the top gem collectors, your top clients, what names
come to mind? Off the top of your head?"

"Oh." Concentrating, she gnawed on her lip. "Peter
Morrison in London, Sylvia Smythe-Simmons of New
York, Henry and Laura Muller here in D.C., Matthew
Wolinski in California. And I suppose Charles Van
Horn here in D.C., too, though he's new to it. We sold
him three lovely stones over the last two years. One

was a spectacular opal I coveted. I'm still hoping he'll let me set it for him. I have this design in my head…."

She shook herself, trailed off when she realized why he was asking. "Lieutenant, I know these people. I've dealt with them personally. The Mullers were friends of my stepfather's. Mrs. Smythe-Simmons is over eighty. None of them are thieves."

He didn't bother to glance up, but continued to write. "Then we'll be able to check them off the list. Taking anything or anyone at face value is a mistake in an investigation, Ms. James. We've had enough mistakes already."

"With mine standing out." Accepting that fact, she nudged her untouched soft drink over the table. "I should have gone to the police right away. I should have turned the information—at the very least, my suspicions—over to the authorities. Several people would still be alive if I had."

"It's possible, but it's not a given." Now he did glance up, noted the haunted look in those soft brown eyes. Compassion stirred. "Did you know your stepbrother was being blackmailed by a second-rate bail bondsman?"

"No," she murmured.

"Did you know that someone was pulling the strings, pulling them hard enough to turn your stepbrother into a killer?"

She shook her head, bit down hard on her lip. "The things I didn't know were the problem, weren't they? I put the two people I love most in terrible danger, then I forgot about them."

"Amnesia isn't a choice, it's a condition. And your friends handled themselves. They still are—in fact, I saw Ms. Fontaine just this morning. She doesn't look any the worse for wear to me."

Bailey caught the disdainful note and turned to face him. "You don't understand her. I would have thought a man who does what you do for a living would be able to see more clearly than that."

He thought he caught a faint hint of pity in her voice, and resented it. "I've always thought of myself as clear-sighted."

"People are rarely clear-sighted when it comes to Grace. They only see what she lets them see—unless they care enough to look deeper. She has the most generous heart of any person I've ever known."

Bailey caught the quick flicker of amused disbelief in his eyes and felt her anger rising against it. Furious, she pushed off the stool. "You don't know anything about her, but you've already dismissed her. Can you conceive of what she's going through right now? Her cousin was murdered—and in her stead."

"She's hardly to blame for that."

"Easy to say. But she'll blame herself, and so will her family. It's easy to blame Grace."

"You don't."

"No, because I know her. And I know she's dealt with perceptions and opinions just like yours most of her life. And her way of dealing with it is to do as she chooses, because whatever she does, those perceptions and opinions rarely change. Right now, she's with her aunt, I imagine, and taking the usual emotional beating."

Her voice heated, became rushed, as emotions swarmed. "Tonight, there'll be a memorial service for Melissa, and the relatives will hammer at her, the way they always do."

"Why should they?"

"Because that's what they do best." Running out of steam she turned her head, looked down at the Three Stars. Love, knowledge, generosity, she thought. Why did it seem there was so little of it in the world? "Maybe you should take another look, Lieutenant Buchanan."

He'd already taken too many, he decided. And he was wasting time. "She certainly inspires loyalty in her friends," he commented. "I'm going to look for those lists."

"You know the way." Dismissing him, Bailey picked up the stones to carry them back to the vault.

* * *

Grace was dressed in black, and had never felt less like grieving. It was six in the evening, and a light rain was beginning to fall. It promised to turn the city into a massive steam room instead of cooling it off. The headache that had been slyly brewing for hours snarled at the aspirin she'd already taken and leaped into full, vicious life.

She had an hour before the wake, one she had arranged quickly and alone, because her aunt demanded it. Helen Fontaine was handling grief in her own way—as she did everything else. In this case, it was by meeting Grace with a cold, damning and dry eye. Cutting off any offer of support or sympathy. And demanding that services take place immediately, and at Grace's expense and instigation.

They would be coming from all points, Grace thought as she wandered the large, empty room, with its banks of flowers, thick red drapes, deep pile carpeting. Because such things were expected, such things were reported in the press. And the Fontaines would never give the public media a bone to pick.

Except, of course, for Grace herself.

It hadn't been difficult to arrange for the funeral home, the music, the flowers, the tasteful canapés. Only phone calls and the invocation of the Fontaine name were required. Helen had brought the photograph herself, the large color print in a shining silver frame that now decorated a polished mahogany table and was flanked with red roses in heavy silver vases that Melissa had favored.

There would be no body to view.

Grace had arranged for Melissa's body to be released from the morgue, had already written the check for the cremation and the urn her aunt had chosen.

There had been no thanks, no acknowledgment. None had been expected.

It had been the same from the moment Helen became her legal guardian. She'd been given the necessities of life—Fontaine-style. Gorgeous homes in several countries to live in, perfectly prepared food, tasteful clothing, an excellent education.

And she'd been told, endlessly, how to eat, how to dress, how to behave, who could be selected as a friend and who could not. Reminded, incessantly, of her good fortune—unearned—in having such a family behind her. Tormented, ruthlessly, by the cousin she was there tonight to mourn, for being orphaned, dependent.

For being Grace.

She'd rebelled against all of it, every aspect, every expectation and demand. She'd refused to be malleable, biddable, predictable. The ache for her parents had eventually dimmed, and with it the child's desperate need for love and acceptance.

She'd given the press plenty to report. Wild parties, unwise affairs, unrestricted spending.

When that didn't ease the hurt, she'd found something else. Something that made her feel decent and whole.

And she'd found Grace.

For tonight, she would be just what her family had come to expect. And she would get through the next endless hours without letting them touch her.

She sat heavily on a sofa with overstuffed velvet seats. Her head pounded, her stomach clutched. Closing her eyes, she willed herself to relax. She would spend this last hour alone, and prepare herself for the rest.

But she'd barely taken the second calming breath when she heard footsteps muffled on the thick patterned carpet. Her shoulders turned to rock, her spine snapped straight. She opened her eyes. And saw Bailey and M.J.

She let her eyes close again, on a pathetic rush of gratitude. "I told you not to come."

"Yeah, like we were going to listen to that." M.J. sat beside her, took her hand.

"Cade and Jack are parking the car." Bailey flanked her other side, took her other hand. "How are you holding up?"

"Better." Tears stung her eyes as she squeezed the hands clasped in hers. "A lot better now."

* * *

On a sprawling estate not so many miles from where Grace sat with those who loved her, a man stared out at the hissing rain.

Everyone had failed, he thought. Many had paid for their failures. But retribution was a poor substitute for the Three Stars.

A delay only, he comforted himself. The Stars were his, they were meant to be his. He had dreamed of them, had held them in his hands in those dreams. Sometimes the hands were human, sometimes not, but they were always his hands.

He sipped wine, watched the rain, and considered his options.

His plans had been delayed by three women. That was humiliating, and they would have to be made to pay for that humiliation.

The Salvinis were dead—Bailey James.

The fools he'd hired to retrieve the second Star were dead—M. J. O'Leary.

The man he'd sent with instructions to acquire the third Star at any cost was dead—Grace Fontaine.

And he smiled. That had been indiscreet, as he'd disposed of the lying fool himself. Telling him there'd been an accident, that the woman had fought him, run from him, and fallen to her death. Telling him he'd searched every corner of the house without finding the stone.

That failure had been irritating enough, but then to discover that the wrong woman had died and that the fool had stolen money and jewels without reporting them. Well, such disloyalty in a business associate could hardly be tolerated.

Smiling dreamily, he took a sparkling diamond earring out of his pocket. Grace Fontaine had worn this on her delectable lobe, he mused. He kept it now as a good-luck charm while he considered what steps to take next.

There were only days left before the Stars would be in the museum. Extracting them from those hallowed halls would take months, if not years, of planning. He didn't intend to wait.

Perhaps he had failed because he had been overcautious, had kept his distance from events. Perhaps the gods required a more personal risk. A more intimate involvement.

It was time, he decided, to step out of the shadows, to meet the women who had kept his property from him, face-to-face. He smiled again, excited by the thought, delighted with the possibilities.

When the knock sounded on the door, he answered with great cheer and good humor. "Enter."

The butler, in stern formal black, ventured no farther than the threshold. His voice held no inflection. "I beg your pardon, Ambassador. Your guests are arriving."

"Very well." He sipped the last of his wine, set the empty crystal flute on a table. "I'll be right down."

When the door closed, he moved to the mirror, examined his flawless tuxedo, the wink of diamond studs, the gleam of the thin gold watch at his wrist. Then he examined his face—the smooth contours, the pampered, pale gold skin, the aristocratic nose, the firm, if somewhat thin, mouth. He brushed a hand over the perfectly groomed mane of silver-threaded black hair.

Then, slowly, smilingly, met his own eyes. Pale, almost translucent blue smiled back. His guests would see what he did, a perfectly groomed man of fifty-two, erudite and educated, well mannered and suave. They wouldn't know what plans and plots he held in his heart. They would see no blood on his hands, though it had been only twenty-four short hours since he used them to kill.

He felt only pleasure in the memory, only delight in the knowledge that he would soon dine with the elite and the influential. And he could kill any one of them with a twist of his hands, with perfect immunity.

He chuckled to himself—a low, seductive sound with shuddering undertones. Tucking the earring back in his pocket, he walked from the room.

The ambassador was mad.

Chapter 5

Seth's first thought when he walked into the funeral parlor was that it seemed more like a tedious cocktail party than like a memorial service. People stood or sat in little cliques and groups, many of them nibbling on canapés or sipping wine. Beneath the strains of a muted Chopin étude, voices murmured. There was an occasional roll or tinkle of laughter.

He heard no tears.

Lights were respectfully dimmed, and set off the glitter and gleam of gems and gold. The fragrance of flowers mixed and merged with the scents worn by both men and women. He saw faces, both elegant and bored.

He saw no grief.

But he did see Grace. She stood looking up into the

face of a tall, slim man whose golden tan set off his golden hair and bright blue eyes. He held one of her hands in his and smiled winningly. He appeared to be speaking quickly, persuasively. She shook her head once, laid a hand on his chest, then allowed herself to be drawn into an anteroom.

Seth's lip curled in automatic disdain. A funeral was a hell of a place for a flirtation.

"Buchanan." Jack Dakota wandered over. He scanned the room, stuck his hands in the pockets of the suit coat he wished fervently was still in his closet, instead of on his back. "Some party."

Seth watched two women air kiss. "Apparently."

"Doesn't seem like one a sane man would want to crash."

"I have business," he said briefly. Which could have waited until morning, he reminded himself. He should have let it wait. It annoyed him that he'd made the detour, that he'd been thinking of Grace—more, that he'd been unable to lock her out of his head.

He pulled a copy of a mug shot out of his pocket, handed it to Jack. "Recognize him?"

Jack scanned the picture, considered. Slick-looking dude, he thought. Vaguely European in looks, with the sleek black hair, dark eyes and refined features. "Nope. Looks like a poster boy for some wussy cologne."

"You didn't see him during your amazing weekend adventures?"

Jack took one last, harder look, handed the shot back. "Nope. What's his connection?"

"His prints were all over the house in Potomac."

Jack's interest rose. "He the one who killed the cousin?"

Seth met Jack's eyes coolly. "That has yet to be determined."

"Don't give me the cop stand, Buchanan. What'd the guy say? He stopped by to sell vacuum cleaners?"

"He didn't say anything. He was too busy floating facedown in the river."

With an oath, Jack's gaze whipped around the room again. He relaxed fractionally when he spotted M.J. huddled with Cade. "The morgue must be getting crowded. You got a name?"

Seth started to dismiss the question. He didn't care for professions that stood a step back from the police. But there was no denying that the bounty hunter and the private investigator were involved. And there was no avoiding the connection, he told himself.

"Carlo Monturri."

"Doesn't ring a bell either."

Seth hadn't expected it would, but the police— on several continents—knew the name. "He's out of your league, Dakota. His type keeps a fancy lawyer on retainer and doesn't use the local bail bondsman to get sprung."

As he spoke, Seth's eyes moved around the room as a cop's did, sweeping corner to corner, taking in details, body language, atmosphere. "Before he took his last swim, he was expensive hired muscle. He worked alone because he didn't like to share the fun."

"Connections in the area?"

"We're working on it."

Seth saw Grace come out of the anteroom. The man who was with her had his arm draped over her shoulders, pulled her close in an intimate embrace, kissed her. The flare of fury kindled in Seth's gut and bolted up to his heart.

"Excuse me."

Grace saw him the moment he started across the room. She murmured something to the man beside her, dislodged him, then dismissed him. Straightening her spine, she fixed on an easy smile.

"Lieutenant, we didn't expect you."

"I apologize for intruding in your—" he flicked a glance toward the golden boy, who was helping himself to a glass a wine "—grief."

The sarcasm slapped, but she didn't flinch. "I assume you have a reason for coming by."

"I'd like a moment of your time—in private."

"Of course." She turned to lead him out and came face-to-face with her aunt. "Aunt Helen."

"If you could tear yourself away from entertaining your suitors," Helen said coldly, "I want to speak to you."

"Excuse me," Grace said to Seth, and stepped into the anteroom again.

Seth debated moving off, giving them privacy. But he stayed where he was, two paces from the doorway. He told himself murder investigations didn't allow for sensitivity. Though they kept their voices low, he heard both women clearly enough.

"I assume you have Melissa's things at your home," Helen began.

"I don't know. I haven't been able to go through the house thoroughly yet."

Helen said nothing for a moment, simply studied her niece through cold blue eyes. Her face was smooth and showed no ravages of grief in the carefully applied makeup. Her hair was sleek, lightened to a tasteful ash blond. Her hands were freshly manicured and glittered with the diamond wedding band she continued to wear, though she'd shared little but her husband's name in over a decade, and a square-cut sapphire given to her by her latest lover.

"I sincerely doubt Melissa came to your home without a bag. I want her things, Grace. All of her things. You'll have nothing of hers."

"I never wanted anything of hers, Aunt Helen."

"Didn't you?" There was a crackle in the voice—a whip flicking. "Did you think she wouldn't tell me of your affair with her husband?"

Grace merely sighed. It was new ground, but sickeningly familiar. Melissa's marriage had failed, publicly. Therefore, it had to be someone else's fault. It had to be Grace's fault.

"I didn't have an affair with Bobbie. Before, during or after their marriage."

"And whom do you think I would believe? You, or my own daughter?"

Grace tilted her head, twisted a smile on her face. "Why, your own daughter, of course. As always."

"You've always been a liar and a sneak. You've always been ungrateful, a burden I took on out of family duty who never once gave anything back. You were spoiled and willful when I opened my door to you, and you never changed."

Grace's stomach roiled viciously. In defense, she smiled, shrugged. Deliberately careless, she smoothed a hand over the hair sleeked into a coiled twist at the nape of her neck. "No, I suppose I didn't. I'll just have to remain a disappointment to you, Aunt Helen."

"My daughter would be alive if not for you."

Grace willed her heart to go numb. But it ached, and it burned. "Yes, you're right."

"I warned her about you, told her time and again what you were. But you continually lured her back, playing on her affection."

"Affection, Aunt Helen?" With a half laugh, Grace pressed her fingers to the throb in her left temple. "Surely even you don't believe she ever had an ounce of affection for me. She took her cue from you, after all. And she took it well."

"How dare you speak of her in that tone, after you've killed her!" In the pampered face, Helen's eyes burned with loathing. "All of your life you've envied her, used your wiles to influence her. Now your unconscionable life-style has killed her. You've brought scandal and disgrace down on the family name once again."

Grace went stiff. This wasn't grief, she thought. Perhaps grief was there, buried deep, but what was on the surface was venom. And she was weary of being struck by it. "That's the bottom line, isn't it, Aunt Helen? The Fontaine name, the Fontaine reputation. And, of course, the Fontaine stock. Your child is dead, but it's the scandal that infuriates you."

She absorbed the slap without a wince, though the blow printed heat on her cheek, brought blood stinging to the surface. She took one long, deep breath. "That should end things appropriately between the two of us," she said evenly. "I'll have Melissa's things sent to you as soon as possible."

"I want you out of here." Helen's voice shook for the first time—whether in grief or in fury, Grace couldn't have said. "You have no place here."

"You're right again. I don't. I never did."

Grace stepped out of the alcove. The color that had drained out of her face rose slightly when she met Seth's eyes. She couldn't read them in that brief glance, and didn't want to. Without breaking stride, she continued past him and kept walking.

The drizzle that misted the air was a relief. She welcomed the heat after the overchilled, artificial air inside, and the heavy, stifling scent of funeral flowers. Her heels clicked on the wet pavement as she crossed the lot to her car. She was fumbling in her bag for her keys when Seth clamped a hand on her shoulder.

He said nothing at first, just turned her around, studied her face. It was white again—but for the red burn from the slap—the eyes a dark contrast and swimming with emotion. He could feel the tremors of that emotion under the palm of his hand.

"She was wrong."

Humiliation was one more blow to her overwrought system. She jerked her shoulder, but his hand remained in place. "Is that part of your investigative technique, Lieutenant? Eavesdropping on private conversations?"

Did she realize, he wondered, that her voice was raw, her eyes were devastated? He wanted badly to lift a hand to that mark on her face, cool it. Erase it. "She was wrong," he said again. "And she was cruel. You aren't responsible."

"Of course I am." She spun away, jabbing her key at the door lock. After three shaky attempts, she gave up, and they dropped with a jingling splash to the wet pavement as she turned into his arms. "Oh, God." Shuddering, she pressed her face into his chest. "Oh, God."

He didn't want to hold her, wanted to refuse the role of comforter. But his arms came around her before he could stop them, and one hand reached up to brush the smooth twist of her hair. "You didn't deserve that, Grace. You did nothing to deserve that."

"It doesn't matter."

"Yes, it does." He found himself weakening, drawing her closer, trying to will her trembling away. "It always does."

"I'm just tired." She burrowed into him while the rain misted her hair. There was strength here, was all she could think. A haven here. An answer here. "I'm just tired."

Her head lifted, their mouths met, before either of them realized the need was there. The quiet sound in her throat was of relief and gratitude. She opened her battered heart to the kiss, locking her arms around him, urging him to take it.

She had been waiting for him, and, too dazed to question why, she offered herself to him. Surely comfort and pleasure and this all-consuming need were reason enough. His mouth was firm—the one she'd always wanted on hers. His body was hard and solid—a perfect match for hers.

Here he is, she thought with a ragged sigh of joy.

She trembled still, and he could feel his own muscles quiver in response. He wanted to gather her up, carry her out of the rain to someplace quiet and dark where it was only the two of them. To spend years where it would only be the two of them.

His heart pounded in his head, masking the slick sound of traffic over the rain-wet street beyond the lot. Its fast, demanding beat muffled the warning struggling to sound in the corner of his brain, telling him to step back, to break away.

He'd never wanted anything more in his life than to bury himself in her and forget the consequences.

Swamped with emotions and needs, she held him close. "Take me home," she murmured against his mouth. "Seth, take me home, make love with me. I need you to touch me. I want to be with you." Her mouth met his again, in a desperate plea she hadn't known herself capable of.

Every cell in his body burned for her. Every need he'd ever had coalesced into one, and it was only for her. The almost vicious focus of it left him vulnerable and shaky. And furious.

He put his hands on her shoulders, drew her away. "Sex isn't the answer for everyone."

His voice wasn't as cool as he'd wanted, but it was rigid enough to stop her from reaching for him again. Sex? she thought as she struggled to clear her dazzled mind. Did he really believe she'd been speaking about something as simple as sex? Then she focused on his face, the hard set of his mouth, the faint annoyance in his eyes, and realized he did.

Her pride might have been tattered, but she managed to hold on to a few threads. "Well, apparently it's not for you." Reaching up, she smoothed her hair, brushed away rain. "Or if it is, you're the type who insists on being the initiator."

She made her lips curve, though they felt cold now and stiff. "It would have been just fine and dandy if you'd made the move. But when I do, it makes me— what would the term be? Loose?"

"I don't believe it's a term I used."

"No, you're much too controlled for insults." She bent down, scooped up her wet keys, then stood jingling them in her hand while she studied him. "But you wanted me right back, Seth. You're not quite controlled enough to have masked that little detail."

"I don't believe in taking everything I want."

"Why the hell not?" She gave a short, mirthless laugh. "We're alive, aren't we? And you, of all people, should know how distressingly short life can be."

"I don't have to explain to you how I live my life."

"No, you don't. But it's obvious you're perfectly willing to question how I live mine." Her gaze skimmed past him, back toward the lights glinting in the funeral home. "I'm quite used to that. I do exactly what I choose, without regard for the consequences. I'm selfish and self-involved and careless."

She lifted a shoulder as she turned and unlocked her door. "As for feelings, why should I be entitled to them?"

She slipped into her car, flipped him one last look. Her mouth might have curved with seductive ease, but the sultry smile didn't reach her eyes, or mask the misery in them. "Well, maybe some other time, handsome."

He watched her drive off into the rain. There would be another time, he admitted, if for no other reason than that he hadn't shown her the picture. Hadn't, he thought, had the heart to add to her unhappiness that night.

Feelings, he mused as he headed to his own car. She

had them, had plenty of them. He only wished he understood them. He got into his car, wrenched his door shut. He wished to God he understood his own.

For the first time in his life, a woman had reached in and clamped a hand on his heart. And she was squeezing.

Seth told himself he wasn't postponing meeting with Grace again. The morning after the memorial service had been hellish with work. And when he did carve out time to leave his office, he'd headed toward M.J.'s. It was true he could have assigned this follow-up to one of his men. Despite the fact that the chief of police had ordered him to head the investigation, and give every detail his personal attention, Mick Marshall—the detective who had taken the initial call on the case—could have done this next pass with M. J. O'Leary.

Seth was forced to admit that he wanted to talk to her personally and hoped to slide a few details out of her on Grace Fontaine.

M.J.'s was a cozy, inviting neighborhood pub that ran to dark woods, gleaming brass and thickly padded stools and booths. Business was slow but steady in midafternoon. A couple of men who looked to be college age were sharing a booth, a duet of foamy mugs and an intense game of chess. An older man sat at the bar working a crossword from the morning paper, and a trio of women with department store shopping bags crowding the floor around them huddled over drinks and laughter.

The bartender glanced at Seth's badge and told him he'd find the boss upstairs in her office. He heard her before he saw her.

"Look, pal, if I'd wanted candy mints, I'd have ordered candy mints. I ordered beer nuts. I want them here by six. Yeah, yeah. I know my customers. Get me the damn nuts, pronto."

She sat behind a crowded desk with a battered top. Her short cap of red hair stood up in spikes. Seth watched her rake her fingers through it again as she hung up the phone and pushed a pile of invoices aside. If that was her idea of filing, he thought, it suited the rest of the room.

It was barely big enough to turn around in, crowded with boxes, files, papers, and one ratty chair, on which sat an enormous and overflowing purse.

"Ms. O'Leary?"

She looked up, her brow still creased in annoyance. It didn't clear when she recognized her visitor. "Just what I needed to make my day perfect. A cop. Listen, Buchanan, I'm behind here. As you know, I lost a few days recently."

"Then I'll try to be quick." He stepped inside, pulled

the picture out of his pocket and tossed it onto the desk under her nose. "Look familiar?"

She pursed her lips, gave the slickly handsome face a slow, careful study. "Is this the guy Jack told me about? The one who killed Melissa?"

"The Melissa Fontaine case is still open. This man is a possible suspect. Do you recognize him?"

She rolled her eyes, pushed the photo back in Seth's direction. "No. Looks like a creep. Did Grace recognize him?"

He angled his head slightly, his only outward sign of interest. "Does she know many men who look like creeps?"

"Too many," M.J. muttered. "Jack said you came by the memorial service last night to show Grace this picture."

"She was…occupied."

"Yeah, it was a rough night for her." M.J. rubbed her eyes.

"Apparently, though she seemed to have been handling it well enough initially." He glanced down at the photo again, thought of the man he'd seen her kiss. "This looks like her type."

M.J.'s hand dropped, her eyes narrowed. "Meaning?"

"Just that." Seth tucked the photo away. "If one's going by type, this one doesn't appear, on the surface, too far a step from the one she was cozy with at the service."

"Cozy with?" The narrowed eyes went hot, angry green flares. "Grace wasn't cozy with anyone."

"About six-one, a hundred and seventy, blond hair, blue eyes, five-thousand-dollar Italian suit, lots of teeth."

It only took her a moment. At any other time, she would have laughed. But the cool disdain on Seth's face had her snarling. "You stupid son of a bitch, that was her cousin Julian, and he was hitting her up for money, just like he always does."

Seth frowned, backtracked, played the scene through his mind again. "Her cousin…and that would be the victim's…?"

"Stepbrother. Melissa's stepbrother—her father's son from a previous."

"And the deceased's stepbrother was asking Grace for money at his stepsister's memorial?"

This time she appreciated the coating of disgust over his words. "Yeah. He's slime—why should the ambience stop him from shaking her down? Most of them squeeze her for a few bucks now and then." She rose, geared up. "And you've got a hell of a nerve coming in here with your attitude and your superior morals, ace. She wrote that pansy-faced jerk a check for a few thousand to get him off her back, just like she used to pass bucks to Melissa, and some of the others."

"I was under the impression the Fontaines were wealthy."

"Wealth's relative—especially if you live the high life and your allowance from your trust fund is over-drawn, or if you've played too deep in Monte Carlo. And Grace has more of the green stuff than most of them, because her parents didn't blow the bucks. That just burns the relatives," she muttered. "Who do you think paid for that wake last night? It wasn't the dearly departed's mama or papa. Grace's witch of an aunt put the arm on her, then put the blame on her. And she took it, because she thinks it's easier to take it and go her own way. You don't know anything about her."

He thought he did, but the details he was collecting bit by bit weren't adding up very neatly. "I know that she's not to blame for what happened to her cousin."

"Yeah, try telling her that. I know that when we re-alized she'd left and we got back to Cade's, she was in her room crying, and there was nothing any of us could do to help her. And all because those bastards she has the misfortune to be related to go out of their way to make her feel rotten."

Not just her relatives, he thought with a quick twinge of guilt. He'd had a part in that.

"It seems she's more fortunate in her friends than in her family."

"That's because we're not interested in her money, or her name. Because we don't judge her. We just love her. Now, if that's all, I've got work to do."

"I need to speak with Ms. Fontaine." Seth's voice was as stiff as M.J.'s had been passionate. "Would you know where I might find her?"

Her lips curled. She hesitated a moment, knowing Grace wouldn't appreciate the information being passed along. But the urge to see the cop's preconceptions slapped down was just too tempting. "Sure. Try Saint Agnes's Hospital. Pediatrics or maternity." Her phone rang, so she snatched it up. "You'll find her," she said. "Yeah, O'Leary," she barked into the phone, and turned her back on Seth.

He assumed she was visiting the child of a friend, but when he asked at the nurses' station for Grace Fontaine, faces lit up.

"I think she's in the intensive care nursery." The nurse on duty checked her watch. "It's her usual time there. Do you know the way?"

Baffled, Seth shook his head. "No." He listened to the directions, while his mind turned over a dozen reasons why Grace Fontaine should have a usual time in a nursery. Since none of them slipped comfortably into a slot, he headed down corridors.

He could hear the high sound of babies crying behind a barrier of glass. And perhaps he stopped for just a moment outside the window of the regular nursery, and his eyes might have softened, just a little, as he scanned the infants in their clear-sided beds. Tiny faces, some slack in sleep, others screwed up into wrinkled balls of fury.

A couple stood beside him, the man with his arm over the woman's robed shoulders. "Ours is third from the left. Joshua Michael Delvecchio. Eight pounds, five ounces. He's one day old."

"He's a beaut," Seth said.

"Which one is yours?" the woman asked.

Seth shook his head, shot one more glance through the glass. "I'm just passing through. Congratulations on your son."

He continued on, resisting the urge to look back at the new parents lost in their own private miracle.

Two turns down the corridor away from the celebration was a smaller nursery. Here machines hummed, and nurses walked quietly. And behind the glass were six empty cribs.

Grace sat beside one, cuddling a tiny, crying baby. She brushed away tears from the pale little cheek, rested her own against the smooth head as she rocked.

It struck him to the core, the picture she made. Her hair was braided back from her face and she wore a shapeless green smock over her suit. Her face was soft as she soothed the restless infant. Her attention was totally focused on the eyes that stared tearfully into hers.

"Excuse me, sir." A nurse hurried up. "This is a restricted area."

Absently, his eyes still on Grace, Seth reached for his badge. "I'm here to speak with Ms. Fontaine."

"I see. I'll tell her you're here, Lieutenant."

"No, don't disturb her." He didn't want anything to spoil that picture. "I can wait. What's wrong with the baby she's holding?"

"Peter's an AIDS baby. Ms. Fontaine arranged for him to have care here."

"Ms. Fontaine?" He felt a fist lodge in his gut. "It's her child?"

"Biologically? No." The nurse's face softened slightly. "I think she considers them all hers. I honestly don't know what we'd do without her help. Not just the foundation, but her."

"The foundation?"

"The Falling Star Foundation. Ms. Fontaine set it up a few years ago to assist critically ill and terminal children and their families. But it's the hands-on that really matters." She gestured back toward the glass with a nod of her head. "No amount of financial generosity can buy a loving touch or sing a lullaby."

He watched the baby calm, drift slowly to sleep in Grace's arms. "She comes here often?"

"As often as she can. She's our angel. You'll have to excuse me, Lieutenant."

"Thank you." As she walked away, he stepped closer to the isolation glass. Grace started toward the crib. It was then that her eyes met his.

He saw the shock come into them first. Even she wasn't skilled enough to disguise the range of emotions that raced over her face. Surprise, embarrassment, annoyance. Then she smoothed the expressions out. Gently, she laid the baby back into the crib, brushed a hand over his cheek. She walked through a side door and disappeared.

It was several minutes before she came out into the corridor. The smock was gone. Now she was a confident woman in a flame-red suit, her mouth carefully tinted to match. "Well, Lieutenant, we meet in the oddest places."

Before she could complete the casual greeting she'd practiced while she tidied her makeup, he took her chin firmly in his hand. His eyes locked intently on hers, probed.

"You're a fake." He said it quietly, stepping closer. "You're a fraud. Who the hell are you?"

"Whatever I like." He unnerved her, that long, intense and all-too-personal study with those golden-brown eyes. "And I don't believe this is the place for an interrogation. I'd like you to let me go now," she said steadily. "I don't want any scenes here."

"I'm not going to cause a scene."

She lifted her brows. "I might." Deliberately she pushed his hand away and started down the corridor. "If you want to discuss the case with me, or have any questions regarding it, we'll do it outside. I won't have it brought in here."

"It was breaking your heart," he murmured. "Holding that baby was breaking your heart."

"It's my heart." Almost viciously, she punched a finger at the button for the elevator. "And it's a tough one, Seth. Ask anyone."

"Your lashes are still wet."

"This is none of your business." Her voice was low and vibrating with fury. "Absolutely none of your business."

She stepped into the crowded elevator, faced front. She wouldn't speak to him about this part of her life, she promised herself. Just the night before, she'd opened herself to him, only to be pushed away, refused. She wouldn't share her feelings again, and certainly not her feelings about something as vital to her as the children.

He was a cop, just a cop. Hadn't she spent several miserable hours the night before convincing herself that was all he was or could be to her? Whatever he stirred in her would have to be stopped—or, if not stopped, at least suppressed.

She would not share with him, she would not trust him, she would not give to him.

By the time she reached the lobby doors, she was steadier. Hoping to shake him quickly, she started toward the lot. Seth merely took her arm, steered her away.

"Over here," he said, and headed toward a grassy area with a pair of benches.

"I don't have time."

"Make time. You're too upset to drive, in any case."

"Don't tell me what I am."

"Apparently that's just what I've been doing. And apparently I've missed several steps. That's not usual for me, and I don't care for it. Sit down."

"I don't want—"

"Sit down, Grace," he repeated. "I apologize."

Annoyed, she sat on the bench, found her sunglasses in her bag and slipped them on. "For?"

He sat beside her, removed the shielding glasses and looked into her eyes. "For not letting myself look beneath the surface. For not wanting to look. And for blaming you because I don't seem able to stop wanting to do this."

He took her face in his hands and captured her mouth with his.

Chapter 6

She didn't move into him. Not this time. Her emotions were simply too raw to risk. Though her mouth yielded beneath his, she lifted a hand and laid it on his chest, as if to keep him at a safe distance.

And still her heart stumbled.

This time she was holding back. He sensed it, felt it in the press of her hand against him. Not refusing, but resisting. And with a knowledge that came from somewhere too deep to measure, he gentled the kiss, seeking not only to seduce, but also to soothe.

And still his heart staggered.

"Don't." It made her throat ache, her mind haze, her body yearn. And it was all too much. She pulled away from him and stood staring out across the little patch of grass until she thought she could breathe again.

"What is it with timing?" Seth wondered aloud. "That makes it so hard to get right?"

"I don't know." She turned then to look at him. He was an attractive man, she decided. The dark hair and hard face, the odd tint of gold in his eyes. But she'd known many attractive men. What was it about this one that changed everything and made her world tilt? "You bother me, Lieutenant Buchanan."

He gave her one of his rare smiles—slow and full and rich. "That's a mutual problem, Ms. Fontaine. You keep me up at night. Like a puzzle where the pieces are all there, but they change shape right before your eyes. And even when you put it all together—or think you have—it doesn't stay the same."

"I'm not a mystery, Seth."

"You are the most fascinating woman I've ever met." His lips curved again when she lifted her brows. "That isn't entirely a compliment. Along with fascination comes frustration." He stood, but didn't step toward her. "Why were you so upset that I found you here, saw you here?"

"It's private." Her tone was stiff again, dismissive. "I go to considerable trouble to keep it private."

"Why?"

"Because I prefer it that way."

"Your family doesn't know about your involvement here?"

The fury that seared through her eyes was burning-cold. "My family has *nothing* to do with this. Nothing. This isn't a Fontaine project, one of their charitable sops for good press and a tax deduction. It's mine."

"Yes, I can see that," he said calmly. Her family had hurt her even more than he'd guessed. And more, he thought, than she had acknowledged. "Why children, Grace?"

"Because they're the innocents." It was out before she realized she meant to say it. Then she closed her eyes and sighed. "Innocence is a precious and perishable commodity."

"Yes, it is. Falling Star? Your foundation. Is that how you see them, stars that burn out and fall too quickly?"

It was her heart he was touching simply by understanding, by seeing what was inside. "It has nothing to do with the case. Why are you pushing me on this?"

"Because I'm interested in you."

She sent him a smile—half inviting, half sarcastic. "Are you? You didn't seem to be when I asked you to bed. But you see me holding a sick baby and you change your tune." She walked toward him slowly, trailed a fingertip down his shirt. "Well, if it's the maternal type that turns you on, Lieutenant—"

"Don't do that to yourself." Again his voice was quiet, controlled. He took her hand, stopped her from backtracking the trail of her finger. "It's foolish. And it's irritating. You weren't playing games in there. You care."

"Yes, I do. I care enormously. And that doesn't make me a hero, and it doesn't make me any different than I was last night." She drew her hand away and stood her ground. "I want you. I want to go to bed with you. That irritates you, Seth. Not the sentiment, but the bluntness of the statement. Isn't it games you'd prefer? That I'd pretend reluctance and let you conquer?"

He only wished it was something just that ordinary. "Maybe I want to know who you are before we end up in bed. I spent a long time looking at your face—that portrait of you in your house. And, looking, I wondered about you. Now, I want you. But I also want all those pieces to fit."

"You might not like the finished product."

"No," he agreed. "I might not."

Then again, she thought… Considering, she angled her head. "I have a thing tonight. A cocktail party hosted by a major contributor to the hospital. I can't afford to skip it. Why don't you take me, then we'll see what happens next?"

He weighed the pros and cons, knew it was a step that would have ramifications he might not be able to handle smoothly. She wasn't simply a woman, and he wasn't simply a man. Whatever was between them had a long reach and a hard grip.

"Do you always think everything through so carefully?" she asked as she watched him.

"Yes." But in her case it didn't seem to matter, he realized. "I can't guarantee my evenings will be free until this case is closed." He shifted times and meetings and paperwork in his head. "But if I can manage it, I'll pick you up."

"Eight's soon enough. If you're not there by quarter after, I'll assume you were tied up."

No complaints, he thought, no demands. Most of the women he'd known shifted to automatic sulk mode when his work took priority. "I'll call if I can't make it."

"Whatever." She sat again, relaxed now. "I don't imagine you came by to see my secret life, or to make a tentative date for a cocktail party." She slipped her sunglasses back on, sat back. "Why are you here?"

He reached inside his jacket for the photo. Grace caught a brief glimpse of his shoulder holster, and the weapon snug inside it. And wondered if he'd ever had occasion to use it.

"I imagine your time is taken up mainly with administration duties." She took the picture from him, but continued to look at Seth's face. "You wouldn't participate in many, what—busts?"

She thought she caught a faint glint of humor in his

eyes, but his mouth remained sober. "I like to keep my hand in."

"Yes," she murmured, easily able to imagine him whipping the weapon out. "I suppose you would."

She shifted her gaze, scanned the face in the photo. This time the humor was in her eyes. "Ah, Joe Cool. Or more likely Juan or Jean-Paul Cool."

"You know him?"

"Not personally, but certainly as a type. He likely speaks the right words in three languages, plays a steely game of baccarat, enjoys his brandy and wears black silk underwear. His Rolex, along with his mono-grammed gold cufflinks and diamond pinkie ring, would have been gifts from admirers."

Intrigued, Seth sat beside her again. "And what are the right words?"

"You're the most beautiful woman in the room. I adore you. My heart sings when I look into your eyes. Your husband is a fool, and darling, you must stop buying me gifts."

"Been there?"

"With some variations. Only I've never been mar-ried and I don't buy trinkets for users. His eyes are cold," she added, "but a lot of women, lonely women, would only see the polish. That's all they want to see." She took a quick, short breath. "This is the man who killed Melissa, isn't it?"

He started to give her the standard response, but she looked up then, and he was close enough to read her eyes through the amber tint of her glasses. "I think it is. His prints were all over the house. Some of the surfaces were wiped, but he missed a lot, which leads me to think he panicked. Either because she fell or because he wasn't able to find what he'd come for."

"And you're leaning toward the second choice, because this isn't the type of man to panic because he'd killed a woman."

"No, he isn't."

"She couldn't have given him what he'd come for. She wouldn't have known what he was talking about."

"No. That doesn't make you responsible. If you indulge yourself by thinking it does, you'd have to blame Bailey, too."

Grace opened her mouth, closed it again, breathed deep. "That's clever logic, Lieutenant," she said after a moment. "So I shed my sackcloth and ashes and blame this man. Have you found him?"

"He's dead." He took the photo back, tucked it away. "And my clever logic leads me to believe that whoever hired him decided to fire him, permanently."

"I see." She felt nothing, no satisfaction, no relief. "So, we're nowhere."

"The Three Stars are under twenty-four-hour guard.

You, M.J. and Bailey are safe, and the museum will have its property in a matter of days."

"And a lot of people have died. Sacrifices to the god?"

"From what I've read about Mithra, it isn't blood he wants."

"Love, knowledge and generosity," she said quietly. "Powerful elements. The diamond I held, it has vitality. Maybe that's the same as power. Does he want them because they're beautiful, priceless, ancient, or because he truly believes in the legend? Does he believe that if he has all of them in their triangle, he'll possess the power of the god, and immortality?"

"People believe what they choose to believe. Whatever reason he wants them, he's killed for them." Staring out across the grass, he stepped over one of his own rules and shared his thoughts with her. "Money isn't the driving force. He's laid out more than a million already. He wants to own them, to hold them in his hands, whatever the cost. It's more than coveting," he said quietly, as a murky scene swam into his mind.

A marble altar, a golden triangle with three brilliantly blue points. A dark man with pale eyes and a bloody sword.

"And you don't think he'll stop now. You think he'll try again."

Baffled and uneasy with the image, he shook it off,

turned back to logic and instinct. "Oh, yeah." Seth's eyes narrowed, went flat. "He'll try again."

Seth made it to Cade's at 8:14. His final meeting of the day, with the chief of police, had gone past seven, and that had barely given him time to get home, change and drive out again. He'd told himself half a dozen times that he'd be better off staying at home, putting the reports and files away and having a quiet evening to relax his mind.

The press conference set for nine sharp the next morning would be a trial by fire, and he needed to be sharp. Yet here he was, sitting in his car feeling ridiculously nervous and unsettled.

He'd tracked a homicidal junkie through a condemned tenement without breaking a sweat, with a steady pulse he'd interrogated cold, vicious killers— but now, as the white ball of the sun dipped low in the sky, he was as jittery as a schoolboy.

He hated cocktail parties. The inane conversations, the silly food, the buffed faces, all feigning enthusiasm or ennui, depending on their style.

But it wasn't the prospect of a few hours socializing with strangers that unnerved him. It was spending time with Grace without the buffer of the job between them.

He'd never had a woman affect him as she did. And he couldn't deny—at least to himself—that he had been deeply, uniquely affected, from the moment he saw her portrait.

It didn't help to tell himself she was shallow, spoiled, a woman used to men falling at her feet. It hadn't helped before he discovered she was much more than that, and it was certainly no good now.

He couldn't claim to understand her, but he was beginning to uncover all those layers and contrasts that made her who and what she was.

And he knew they would be lovers before the night was over.

He saw her step out of the house, a charge of electric blue from the short strapless dress molded to her body, the long, luxurious fall of ebony hair, the endless and perfect legs.

Did she shock every man's system, Seth wondered, just the look of her? Or was he particularly, specifically vulnerable? He decided either answer would be hard to live with, and got out of his car.

Her head turned at the sound of his door, and that heart-stopping face bloomed with a smile. "I didn't think you were going to make it." She crossed to him, unhurried, and touched her mouth to his. "I'm glad you did."

"I'd said I'd call if I wouldn't be here."

"So you did." But she hadn't counted on it. She'd left the address of the party inside, just in case, but she'd resigned herself to spending the evening without him. She smiled again, smoothed a hand down the lapel of his suit. "I never wait by the phone. We're going to Georgetown. Shall we take my car, or yours?"

"I'll drive." Knowing she expected him to make some comment on her looks, he deliberately kept silent as he walked around the car to open her door.

She slipped in, her legs sliding silkily inside. He wanted his hands there, right there where the abbreviated hem of her dress kissed her thighs. Where the skin would be tender as a ripened peach and smooth as white satin.

He closed the door, walked back around the car and got behind the wheel. "Where in Georgetown?" was all he said.

It was a beautiful old house, with soaring ceilings, heavy antiques and deep, warm colors. The lights blazed down on important people, people of influence and wealth, who carried the scent of power under their perfumes and colognes.

She belonged, Seth thought. She'd melded with the whole from the moment she stepped through the door to exchange sophisticated cheek brushes with the hostess.

Yet she stood apart. In the midst of all the sleek

black, the fussy pastels, she was a bright blue flame daring anyone to touch and be burned.

Like the diamonds, he thought. Unique, potent... irresistible.

"Lieutenant Buchanan, isn't it?"

Seth shifted his gaze from Grace and looked at the short, balding man who was built like a boxer and dressed in Savile Row. "Yes. Mr. Rossi, counsel for the defense. If the defense has deep enough pockets."

Unoffended, Rossi chuckled. "I thought I recognized you. I've crossed you on the stand a few times. You're a tough nut. I've always believed I'd have gotten Tremaine off, or at least hung the jury, if I'd have been able to shake your testimony."

"He was guilty."

"As sin," Rossi agreed readily, "but I'd have hung that jury."

As Rossi started to rehash the trial, Seth resigned himself to talking shop.

Across the room, Grace took a glass from a passing waiter and listened to her hostess's gossip with half an ear. She knew when to chuckle, when to lift a brow, purse her lips, make some interesting comment. It was all routine.

She wanted to leave immediately. She wanted to get Seth out of that dark suit. She wanted her hands on him, all over him. Lust was creeping along her skin

like a hot rash. Sips of champagne did nothing to cool
her throat, and only added to the bubbling in her blood.

"My dear Sarah."

"Gregor, how lovely to see you."

Grace shifted, sipped, smiled at the sleek, dark man
with the creamy voice who bent gallantly over their
hostess's hand. Mediterranean, she judged, by the
charm of the accent. Fiftyish, but fit.

"You're looking particularly wonderful tonight," he
said, lingering over her hand. "And your hospitality, as
always, is incomparable. And your guests." He turned
smiling pale silvery-blue eyes on Grace. "Perfect."

"Gregor." Sarah simpered, fluttered, then turned
to Grace. "I don't believe you've met Gregor, Grace.
He's fatally charming, so be very careful. Ambassador DeVane, I'd like to present Grace Fontaine, a dear
friend."

"I am honored." He lifted Grace's hand, and his lips
were warm and soft. "And enchanted."

"Ambassador?" Grace slipped easily into the role.
"I thought ambassadors were old and stodgy. All the
ones I've met have been. That is, up until now."

"I'll just leave you with Grace, Gregor. I see we have
some late arrivals."

"I'm sure I'm in delightful hands." With obvious reluctance, he released Grace's fingers. "Are you perhaps
a connection of Niles Fontaine?"

"He's an uncle, yes."

"Ah. I had the pleasure of meeting your uncle and his charming wife in Capri a few years ago. We have a mutual hobby, coins."

"Yes, Uncle Niles has quite a collection. He's mad for coins." Grace brushed her hair back, lifted it off her bare shoulder. "And where are you from, Ambassador DeVane?"

"Gregor, please, in such friendly surroundings. Then I might be permitted to call you Grace."

"Of course." Her smile warmed to suit the new intimacy.

"I doubt you would have heard of my tiny country. We are only a small dot in the sea, known chiefly for our olive oil and wine."

"Terresa?"

"Now I am flattered again that such a beautiful woman would know my humble country."

"It's a beautiful island. I was there briefly, two years ago, and very much enjoyed it. Terresa is a small jewel in the sea, dramatic cliffs to the west, lush vineyards in the east, and sandy beaches as fine as sugar."

He smiled at her, took her hand again. The connection was as unexpected as the woman, and he found himself compelled to touch. And to keep. "You must promise to return, to allow me to show you the country as it should be seen. I have a small villa in the west, and the view would almost be worthy of you."

"I'd love to see it. How difficult it must be to spend the summer in muggy Washington, when you could be enjoying the sea breezes of Terresa."

"Not at all difficult. Now." He skimmed a thumb over her knuckles. "I find the treasures of your country more and more appealing. Perhaps you would consider joining me one evening. Do you enjoy the opera?"

"Very much."

"Then you must allow me to escort you. Perhaps—" He broke off, a flicker of annoyance marring his smooth features as Seth stepped up to them.

"Ambassador Gregor DeVane of Terresa, allow me to introduce Lieutenant Seth Buchanan."

"You are military," DeVane said, offering a hand.

"Cop," Seth said shortly. He didn't like the ambassador's looks. Not one bit. When he saw DeVane with Grace, he'd had a fast, turbulent impulse to reach for his weapon. But, strangely, his instinctive movement hadn't been up, to his gun, but lower on the side. Where a man would carry a sword.

"Ah, the police." DeVane blinked in surprise, though he already had a full dossier on Seth Buchanan. "How fascinating. I hope you'll forgive me for saying it's my fondest wish never to require your services." Smoothly DeVane slipped a glass from a passing tray, handed it to Seth, then took one for himself. "But perhaps we should drink to crime. Without it, you'd be obsolete."

Seth eyed him levelly. There was recognition, inexplicable, and utterly adversarial, when their eyes locked, pale silver to dark gold. "I prefer drinking to justice."

"Of course. To the scales, shall we say, and their constant need for balancing?" Gregor drank, then inclined his head. "You'll excuse me, Lieutenant Buchanan, I've yet to greet my host. I was—" he turned to Grace and kissed her hand again "—beautifully distracted from my duty."

"It was a pleasure to meet you, Gregor."

"I hope to see you again." He looked deeply into her eyes, held the moment. "Very soon."

The moment he turned away, Grace shivered. There had been something almost possessive in that last, long stare. "What an odd and charming man," she murmured.

Energy was shooting through Seth, the need to do battle. His system sparked with it. "Do you usually let odd and charming men drool over you in public?"

It was small of her, Grace supposed, but she enjoyed a kick of satisfaction at the annoyance in Seth's tone. "Of course. Since I so dislike them drooling over me in private." She turned into him, so that their bodies brushed lightly. Then slanted a look up from under that thick curtain of lashes. "You don't plan to drool, do you?"

He could have damned her for shooting his system from slow burn up to sizzle. "Finish your drink," he said abruptly, "and say your goodbyes. We're going."

Grace gave an exaggerated sigh. "Oh, I do love being dominated by a strong man."

"We're about to put that to the test." He took her half-finished drink, set it aside. "Let's go."

DeVane watched them leave, studied the way Seth pressed a hand to the small of Grace's back to steer her through the crowd. He would have to punish the cop for touching her.

Grace was his property now, DeVane thought as he gritted his teeth painfully tight to suppress the rage. She was meant for him. He'd known it from the moment he took her hand and looked into her eyes. She was perfect, flawless. It wasn't just the Three Stars that were fated for him, but the woman who had held one, perhaps caressed it, as well.

She would understand their power. She would add to it.

Along with the Three Stars of Mithra, DeVane vowed, Grace Fontaine would be the treasure of his collection.

She would bring the Stars to him. And then she would belong to him. Forever.

* * *

As she stepped outside, Grace felt another shudder sprint down her spine. She hunched her shoulder blades against it, looked back. Through the tall windows filled with light she could see the guests mingling.

And she saw DeVane, quite clearly. For a moment, she would have sworn their eyes met—but this time there was no charm. An irrational sense of fear lodged in her stomach, had her turning quickly away again.

When Seth pulled open the car door, she got in without complaint or comment. She wanted to go, to get away from those brilliantly lit windows and the man who seemed to watch her from beyond them. Briskly she rubbed the chill from her arms.

"You wouldn't be cold if you'd worn clothes." Seth stuck the key in the ignition.

The single remark, issued with cold and savage control, made her chuckle and chased the chill away. "Why, Lieutenant, and here I was wondering how long you would let me keep on what I am wearing."

"Not a hell of a lot longer," he promised, and pulled out into the street.

"Good." Determined to see that he kept that promise, she squirmed over and began to nibble his ear. "Let's break some laws," she whispered.

"I could already charge myself with intent."

She laughed again, quick, breathless, and had him hard as iron.

He wasn't sure how he managed to handle the car, much less drive it through traffic out of D.C. and back into Maryland. She worked his tie off, undid half the buttons of his shirt. Her hands were everywhere, and her mouth teased his ear, his neck, his jaw, while she murmured husky promises, suggestions.

The fantasies she wove with unerring skill had the blood beating painfully in his loins.

He pulled to a jerky stop in his driveway, then dragged her across the seat. She lost one shoe in the car and the other halfway up the walk as he half carried her. Her laughter, dark, wild, damning, roared in his head. He all but broke his own door down to get her inside. The instant they were, he pushed her back against the wall and savaged her mouth.

He wasn't thinking. Couldn't think. It was all primal, violent need. In the darkened hallway, he hiked up her skirt with impatient hands, found the thin, lacy barrier beneath and ripped it aside. He freed himself, then, gripping her hips, plunged into her where they stood.

She cried out, not in protest, not in shock at the almost brutal treatment. But in pure, overwhelming pleasure. She locked herself around him, let him drive her ruthlessly, crest after torrential crest. And met him thrust for greedy, desperate thrust.

It was mindless and hot and vicious. And it was all that mattered. Sheer animal need. Violent animal release.

Her body shattered, went limp, as she felt him pour into her.

He slapped his hand against the wall to keep his balance, struggled to slow his breathing, clear his fevered brain. They were no more than a step inside his door, he realized, and he'd mounted her like a rutting bull.

There was no point in apologies, he thought. They'd both wanted fast and urgent. No, *wanted* was too tame a word, he decided. They'd craved it, the way starving animals craved meat.

But he'd never treated a woman with less care, or so completely ignored the consequences.

"I meant to get you out of that dress," he managed, and was pleased when she laughed.

"We'll get around to it."

"There's something else I didn't get around to." He eased back, studied her face in the dim light. "Is that going to be a problem?"

She understood. "No." And though it was rash and foolish, she felt a twinge of regret that there would be no quickening of life inside her as a result of their carelessness. "I take care of myself."

"I didn't want this to happen." He took her chin in his hand. "I should have been able to keep my hands off you."

Her eyes glimmered in the dark—confident and amused. "I hope you don't expect me to be sorry you didn't. I want them on me again. I want mine on you."

"While they are." He lifted her chin a little higher. "No one else's are. I don't share."

Her lips curved slowly as she kept his gaze. "Neither do I."

He nodded, accepting. "Let's go upstairs," he said, and swept her into his arms.

Chapter 7

He switched on the light as he carried her into his room. This time he needed to see her, to know when her eyes clouded or darkened, to witness those flickers of pleasure or shock.

This time he would remember man's advantage over the animal, and that the mind and heart could play a part.

She got a sense of a room of average size, simple buff-colored curtains at the windows, clean-lined furniture without color, a large bed with a navy spread tucked in with precise, military tidiness.

There were paintings on the walls that she told herself she would study later, when her heart wasn't skipping. Scenes both urban and rural were depicted in misty, dreamy watercolors that made a personal contrast to the practical room.

But all thoughts of art and decor fled when he set her on her feet beside the bed. She reached out, undid the final buttons of his shirt, while he shrugged out of his jacket. Her brows lifted when she noted he wore his shoulder holster.

"Even to a cocktail party?"

"Habit," he said simply, and took it off, hung it over a chair. He caught the look in her eye. "Is it a problem?"

"No. I was just thinking how it suits you. And wondering if you look as sexy putting it on as you do taking it off." Then she turned, scooped her hair over her shoulder. "I could use some help."

He let his gaze wander over her back. Instead of reaching for the zipper, he drew her against him and lowered his mouth to her bare shoulder. She sighed, tipped her head back.

"That's even better."

"Round one took the edge off," he murmured, then slid his hands around her waist, and up, until they cupped her breasts. "I want you whimpering, wanting, weak."

His thumbs brushed the curves just above the bold blue silk. Focused on the sensation, she reached back, linked her arms around his neck. Her body began to move, timed to his strokes, but when she tried to turn, he held her in place.

She moaned, shifted restlessly, when his fingers curved under her bodice, the backs teasing her nipples, making them heat and ache. "I want to touch you."

"Whimpering," he repeated, and ran his hands down her dress to the hem, then beneath. "Wanting." And cupped her. "Weak." Pierced her.

The orgasm flooded her, one long, slow wave that swamped the senses. The whimper he'd waited for shuddered through her lips.

He toed off his shoes, then lowered her zipper inch by inch. His fingers barely brushed her skin as he spread the parted material, eased it down her body until it pooled at her feet. He turned her, stepped back.

She wore only a garter, in the same hot blue as the dress, with stockings so sheer they appeared to be little more than mist. Her body was a fantasy of generous curves, and satin skin. Her hair fell like wild black rain over her shoulders.

"Too many men have told you you're beautiful for it to matter that I say it."

"Just tell me you want me. That matters."

"I want you, Grace." He stepped to her again, took her into his arms, but instead of the greedy kiss she'd expected, he gave her one to slowly drown in. Her arms clutched around him, then went limp, at this new assault to the senses.

"Kiss me again," she murmured when his lips wandered to her throat. "Just like that. Again."

So his mouth met hers, let her sink a second time. With a dreamy hum of pleasure, she slipped his shirt away, let her hands explore. It was lovely to be savored, to be given the gift of a slow kindling flame, to feel the control slip out of her hands into his. And to trust.

He let himself learn her body inch by generous inch. Pleasured them both by possessing those full firm breasts, first with hands, then with mouth. He lowered his hands, flicked the hooks of her stockings free one by one—hearing her quick catch of breath each time. Then slid his hands under the filmy fabric to flesh.

Warm, smooth. He lowered her to the bed, felt her body yield beneath his. Soft, willing. Her lips answered his. Eager, generous.

They watched each other in the light. Moved together. First a sigh, then a groan. She found muscle, the rough skin of an old scar, and the taste of man. Shifting, she drew his slacks down, feasted on his chest as she undressed him. When he took her breasts again, pulled her closer to suckle, her arms quivered and her hair drifted forward to curtain them both.

She felt the heat rising, sliding through her blood like a fever, until her breath was short and shallow.

She could hear herself saying his name, over and over, as he patiently built her toward the edge.

Her eyes went cobalt, fascinating him. Her pillowsoft lips trembled, her glorious body quaked. Even as the need for release clawed at him, he continued to savor. Until he finally shifted her to her back and, with his eyes locked on hers, buried himself inside her.

She arched upward, her hands fisting in the sheets, her body stunned with pleasure. "Seth." Her breath expelled in a rush, burned her lungs. "It's never... Not like this. Seth—"

Before she could speak again, he closed her mouth with his and took her.

When sleep came, Grace dreamed she was in her garden in the mountains, with the woods, thick and green and cool, surrounding her. The hollyhocks loomed taller than her head and bloomed in deep, rich reds and clear, shimmering whites. A hummingbird, shimmering sapphire and emerald, drank from a trumpet flower. Cosmos and coneflowers, dahlias and zinnias made a cheerful wave of mixed colors.

Pansies turned their exotic little faces toward the sun and smiled.

Here she was happy, at peace with herself. Alone, but never lonely. Here there was no sound but the song of the breeze through the leaves, the hum of bees, the faint music of the creek bubbling over rocks.

She watched deer walk quietly out of the woods to drink from the slow-moving creek, their hooves lost in the low-lying mist that hugged the ground. The dawn light shimmered like silver, sparkled off the soft dew, caught rainbows in the mist.

Content, she walked through her flowers, fingers brushing blooms, scents rising up to please her senses. She saw the glint among the blossoms, the bright, beckoning blue, and, stooping, plucked the stone from the ground.

Power shimmered in her hand. It was a clean, flowing sensation, pure as water, potent as wine. For a moment, she stood very still, her hand open. The stone resting in her palm danced with the morning light.

Hers to guard, she thought. To protect. And to give.

When she heard the rustle in the woods, she turned, smiling. It would be him, she was certain. She'd waited for him all her life, wanted so desperately to welcome him, to walk into his arms and know they would wrap around her.

She stepped forward, the stone warming her palm, the faint vibrations from it traveling like music up her arm and toward her heart. She would give it to him, she thought. She would give him everything she had, everything she was. For love had no boundaries.

All at once, the light changed, hazed over. The air went cold and whipped with the wind. By the creek, the deer lifted their heads, alert, alarmed, then turned as one and fled into the sheltering trees. The hum of bees died into a rumble of thunder, and lightning snaked over the dingy sky.

There in the darkened wood, close, too close to where her flowers bloomed, something moved stealthily. Her fingers clutched reflexively, closing fast over the stone. And through the leaves she saw eyes, bright, greedy. And watching.

The shadows parted and opened the path to her.

"No." Frantic, Grace pushed at the hands that held her. "I won't give it to you. It's not for you."

"Easy." Seth pulled her up, stroked her hair. "Just a nightmare. Shake it off now."

"Watching me…" She moaned it, pressed her face into his strong, bare shoulder, drew in his scent and was soothed. "He's watching me. In the woods, watching me."

"No, you're here with me." Her heart was pounding hard enough to bring real concern. Seth tightened his grip, as if to slow it and block the tremors that shook her. "It's a dream. There's no one here but me. I've got you."

"Don't let him touch me. I'll die if he touches me."

"I won't." He tipped her face back. "I've got you," he repeated, and warmed her trembling lips with his.

"Seth." Relief shuddered through her as she clutched at him. "I was waiting for you. In the garden, waiting for you."

"Okay. I'm here now." To protect, he thought. And then to cherish. Shaken by the depth of that, he eased her backward, brushed the tumbled hair away from her face. "Must have been a bad one. Do you have a lot of nightmares?"

"What?" Disoriented, trapped between the dream and the present, she only stared at him.

"Do you want the light?" He didn't wait for an answer, but reached around her to switch on the bedside lamp. Grace turned her face away from the glare, pressed her fisted hand against her heart. "Relax now. Come on." He took her hand, started to open her fingers.

"No." She jerked it back. "He wants it."

"Wants what?"

"The Star. He's coming for it, and for me. He's coming."

"Who?"

"I don't… I don't know." Baffled now, she looked down at her hand, slowly opened it. "I was holding the stone." She could still feel the heat, the weight. "I had it. I found it."

"It was a dream. The diamonds are locked in a vault. They're safe." He tipped a finger under her chin until her eyes met his. "You're safe."

"It was a dream." Saying it aloud brought both relief and embarrassment. "I'm sorry."

"It's all right." He studied her, saw that her face was white, her eyes were fragile. Something moved inside him, shifted, urged his hand to reach out, stroke that pale cheek. "You've had a rough few days, haven't you?"

It was just that, the quiet understanding in his voice, that had her eyes filling. She closed them to will back the tears and took careful breaths. The pressure in her chest was unbearable. "I'm going to get some water."

He simply reached out and drew her in. She'd hidden all that fear and grief and weariness inside her very well, he realized. Until now. "Why don't you let it go?"

Her breath hitched, tore. "I just need to—"

"Let it go," he repeated, and settled her head on his shoulder.

She shuddered once, then clung. Then wept.

He offered no words. He just held her.

At eight the next morning, Seth dropped her off at Cade's. She'd protested the hour at which he shook her out of sleep, tried to curl herself into the mattress. He'd dealt with that by simply picking her up, carrying her into the shower and turning it on. Cold.

He'd given her exactly thirty minutes to pull herself together, then packed her into the car.

"The gestapo could have taken lessons from you," she commented as he pulled up behind M.J.'s car. "My hair's still wet."

"I didn't have the hour to spare it must take to dry all that."

"I didn't even have time to put my makeup on."

"You don't need it."

"I suppose that's your idea of a compliment."

"No, it's just a fact."

She turned to him, looking arousing, rumpled and erotic in the strapless dress. "You, on the other hand, look all pressed and tidy."

"I didn't take twenty minutes in the shower." She'd sung in the shower, he remembered. Unbelievably off-key. Thinking of it made him smile. "Go away. I've got work to do."

She pouted, then reached for her purse. "Well, thanks for the lift, Lieutenant." Then laughed when he pushed her back against the seat and gave her the long, thorough kiss she'd been hoping for.

"That almost makes up for the one miserly cup of coffee you allowed me this morning." She caught his bottom lip between her teeth, and her eyes sparkled into his. "I want to see you tonight."

"I'll come by. If I can."

"I'll be here." She opened the door, shot him a look over her shoulder. "If I can."

Unable to resist, he watched her every sauntering step toward the house. The minute she closed the front door behind her, he shut his eyes.

My God, he thought, he was in love with her. And it was totally impossible.

Inside, Grace all but danced down the hall. She was in love. And it was glorious. It was new and fresh and the first. It was what she'd been waiting for her entire life. Her face glowed as she stepped into the kitchen and found Bailey and Cade at the table, sharing coffee.

"Good morning, troops." She all but sang it as she headed to the coffeepot.

"Good morning to you." Cade tucked his tongue in his cheek. "I like your pajamas."

Laughing, she carried her cup to the table, then leaned down and kissed him full on the mouth. "I just adore you. Bailey, I just adore this man. You'd better snap him up quick, before I get ideas."

Bailey smiled dreamily into her coffee, then looked up, eyes shining and damp. "We're getting married in two weeks."

"What?" Grace bobbled her mug, sloshed coffee

dangerously close to the rim. "What?" she repeated, and sat heavily.

"He won't wait."

"Why should I?" Reaching over the table, Cade took Bailey's hand. "I love you."

"Married." Grace looked down at their joined hands. A perfect match, she thought, and let out a shaky sigh. "That's wonderful. That's incredibly wonderful." Laying a hand over theirs, she stared into Cade's eyes. And saw exactly what she needed to see. "You'll be good to her." It wasn't a question, it was acceptance.

After giving his hand a quick squeeze, she sat back. "Well, a wedding to plan, and a whole two weeks to do it. That ought to make us all insane."

"It's just going to be a small ceremony," Bailey began. "Here at the house."

"I'm going to say one word." Cade put a plea in his voice. *"Elopement."*

"No." With a shake of her head, Bailey drew back, picked up her mug. "I'm not going to start our life together by insulting your family."

"They're not human. You can't insult the inhuman. Muffy will bring the beasts with her."

"Don't call your niece and nephew beasts."

"Wait a minute." Grace held up a hand. Her brows knit. "Muffy? Is that Muffy Parris Westlake? She's your sister?"

"Guilty."

Grace managed to suppress most of the snort of laughter. "That would make Doro Parris Lawrence your other sister." She rolled her eyes, picturing the two annoying and self-important Washington hostesses. "Bailey, run for your life. Go to Vegas. You and Cade can get married by a nice Elvis-impersonator judge and have a delightful, quiet life in the desert. Change your names. Never come back."

"See?" Pleased, Cade slapped a hand on the table. "She knows them."

"Stop it, both of you." Bailey refused to laugh, though her voice trembled with it. "We'll have a small, dignified ceremony—with Cade's family." She smiled at Grace. "And mine."

"Keep working on her." Cade rose. "I've got a couple things to do before I go into the office."

Grace picked up her coffee again. "I don't know his family well," she told Bailey. "I've managed to avoid that little pleasure, but I can tell you from what I do know, you've got the cream of the crop."

"I love him so much, Grace. I know it's all happened quickly, but—"

"What does time have to do with it?" Because she knew they were both about to get teary, she leaned forward. "We have to discuss the important, the vital, aspects of this situation, Bailey." She took a deep breath. "When do we go shopping?"

M.J. staggered in to the sound of laughter, and scowled at both of them. "I hate cheerful people in the morning." She poured coffee, tried to inhale it, then turned to study Grace. "Well, well," she said dryly. "Apparently you and the cop got to know each other last night."

"Well enough that I know he's more than a badge and an attitude." Irritated, she pushed her mug aside. "What have you got against him?"

"Other than the fact he's cold and arrogant, superior and stiff, nothing at all. Jack says they call him the Machine. Small wonder."

"I always find it interesting," Grace said coolly, "when people only skim the surface, then judge another human being. All those traits you just listed describe a man you don't know."

"M.J., drink your coffee." Bailey rose to get the cream. "You know you're not fit to be around until you've had a half a gallon."

M.J. shook her head, fisted a hand on a hip covered with a tattered T-shirt and equally tattered shorts. "Just because you slept with him, doesn't mean you know him, either. You're usually a hell of a lot more careful than that, Grace. You might let other people assume you pop into bed with a new guy every other night, but we know better. What the hell were you thinking of?"

"I was thinking of *me,*" she shot back. "I wanted him. I needed him. He's the first man who's ever really touched me. And I'm not going to let you stand there and make something beautiful into something cheap."

No one spoke for a moment. Bailey stood near the table, the creamer in one hand. M.J. slowly straightened from the counter, whistled out a breath. "You're falling for him." Staggered, she raked a hand through her hair. "You're really falling for him."

"I've already hit the ground with a splat. So what?"

"I'm sorry." M.J. struggled to adjust. She didn't have to like the man, she told herself. She just had to love Grace. "There must be something to him, if he got to you. Are you sure you're okay with it?"

"No, I'm not sure I'm okay with it." Temper drained, and doubt snuck in. "I don't know why it's happened or what to do about it. I just know it is. It wasn't just sex." She remembered how he had held her while she cried. How he'd left the light on for her without her having to ask. "I've been waiting for him all my life."

"I know what that means." Bailey set the creamer down, took Grace's hand. "Exactly."

"So do I." With a sigh, M.J. stepped forward. "What's happening to us? We're three sensible women, and suddenly we're guarding ancient mythical stones, running from bad guys and falling headlong into love with men we've just met. It's crazy."

"It's right," Bailey said quietly. "You know it feels right."

"Yeah." M.J. laid her hand over theirs. "I guess it does."

It wasn't easy for Grace to go back into her house. This time, though, she wasn't alone. M.J. and Jack flanked her like bookends.

"Man." Scanning the wreck of the living area, M.J. hissed out a breath. "I thought they did a number on my place. Of course, you've got a lot more toys to play with."

Then her gaze focused on the splintered railing. And the outline below. "You don't want to do this now, Grace."

"The police cleared the scene. I have to get started on it sometime."

M.J. shook her head. "Where?"

"I'll start in the bedroom." Grace managed a smile. "I'm about to make my dry cleaner a millionaire."

"I'll see what I can do with the railing," Jack told her. "Jury-rig something so it's safe until you have it rebuilt."

"I'd appreciate it."

"Go on up," M.J. suggested. "I'll get a broom. And a

bulldozer." She waited until Grace was upstairs before she turned to Jack. "I'm going to do this down here. Get rid of…things." Her gaze wandered to the outline. "She shouldn't have to handle that."

He leaned down to kiss her forehead. "You're a stand-up pal, M.J."

"Yeah, that's me." She inhaled sharply. "Let's see if we can dig up the stereo or the TV out of this mess. I could use some racket in here."

It took most of the afternoon before Grace was satisfied that the house was cleared out enough to call in her cleaning service. She wanted every room scrubbed before she lived there again.

And she was determined to do just that. To live, to be at home, to face whatever ghosts remained. To prove to herself that she could, she separated from M.J. and Jack and went shopping for the first replacements. Then, because the entire day had left her feeling raw, she stopped by Salvini.

She needed to see Bailey.

And she needed to see the Stars.

Once she was buzzed in, she found Bailey up in her office on the phone. With a smile, Bailey gestured her in. "Yes, Dr. Linstrum, I'm faxing the report to you now, and I'll bring you the original personally before five. I can complete the final tests you've ordered tomorrow."

She listened a moment, ran a finger down the soapstone elephant on her desk. "No, I'm fine. I appreciate your concern, and your understanding. The Stars are my priority. I'll have full copies of all the reports for your insurance carrier by end of business day Friday. Yes, thank you. Goodbye."

"You're working very quickly," Grace commented.

"Despite all that happened, hardly any time was lost. And everyone will feel more comfortable when the stones are in the museum."

"I want to see them again, Bailey." She let out a little laugh. "It's silly, but I really need to. I had this dream last night—nightmare, really."

"What kind of dream?"

Grace sat on the edge of the desk and told her. Though her voice was steady, her fingers tapped with nerves.

"I had dreams, too," Bailey murmured. "I'm still having them. So is M.J."

Uneasy, Grace shifted. "Like mine?"

"Similar enough to be more than coincidence." She rose, held out a hand for Grace's. "Let's go take a look."

"You're not breaking any laws, are you?"

As they walked downstairs together, Bailey sent her an amused look. "I think after what I've already done, this is a minor infraction." She tried to block it, but a shudder escaped as they descended the last flight of steps, under which she'd once hidden from a killer.

"Are you going to be all right here?" Instinctively Grace hooked an arm around Bailey's shoulder. "I hate thinking of what happened, and now thinking of you working here, remembering it."

"It's getting better. Grace, I've had my stepbrothers cremated. Or rather, Cade took care of the arrangements. He wouldn't let me handle any of it."

"Good for him. You don't owe them anything, Bailey. You never did. We're your family. We always will be."

"I know."

She passed into the vault room and approached the massive reinforced-steel doors. The security system was complex and intricate, and even with the ease of long practice, it took Bailey three full minutes to disengage.

"Maybe I ought to have one of these installed in my house," Grace said lightly. "That bastard popped my library safe like it was a gumball machine. He must have fenced the jewelry fast. I hate losing the pieces you made for me."

"I'll make you more. In fact—" Bailey picked up a square velvet box "—let's start now."

Curious, Grace opened the box to a pair of heavy

gold earrings. The smooth crescent-shaped gold was studded with stones in deep, dark hues of emerald, ruby and sapphire.

"Bailey, they're beautiful."

"I'd just finished them before...well, before. As soon as I had, I knew they were yours."

"It's not my birthday."

"I thought you were dead." Bailey's voice shook, then strengthened when Grace looked up. "I thought I would never see you again. So let's consider these a celebration of the rest of our lives."

Grace removed the simple studs in her ears, began to replace them with Bailey's gift. "When I'm not wearing them, I'll keep them with my mother's jewelry. The things that matter most."

"They look perfect on you. I knew they would." Bailey turned, took the heavy padded box from its shelf in the vault. Holding it between them, she opened it.

Grace let out a long, uneven sigh. "I honestly thought one would be gone. I would drive up to the mountains and find it in my garden, sitting on the ground beneath the flowers. It was so real, Bailey."

Reaching out, Grace took a stone. Her stone. "I felt it in my hand, just as I do now. It pulsed in my hand like a heart." She laughed a little, but the sound was hollow. "My heart. That's what it seemed like. I didn't realize that until now. It was like holding my own heart."

"There's a link." A little pale, Bailey took another stone from the box. "I don't understand it, but I know it. This is the Star I had. If M.J. was here, she'd have picked hers."

"I never thought I believed in this sort of thing." Grace turned the stone in her hand. "I was wrong. It's incredibly easy to believe it. To know it. Are we protecting them, Bailey, or are they protecting us?"

"I like to think it's both. They brought me Cade." Gently, she replaced her stone, touched a fingertip to the second Star in its hollow. "Brought M.J. Jack." Her face softened. "I opened up the showroom for them a little while ago," she told Grace. "Jack dragged her in and bought her a ring."

"A ring?" Grace lifted a hand to her heart as it swelled. "An engagement ring?"

"An engagement ring. She argued the whole time, kept telling him not to be a jerk. She didn't need any ring. He just ignored her and pointed to this lovely green tourmaline—square-cut, with diamond baguettes. I designed it a few months ago, thinking that it would make a wonderful, nontraditional engagement ring for the right woman. He knew she was the right woman."

"He's perfect for her." Grace brushed a tear from her lashes and beamed. "I knew it as soon as I saw them together."

"I wish you'd seen them today. There she is, grumbling, rolling her eyes, insisting all this fuss is a waste of time and effort. Then he put that ring on her finger. She got this big, sloppy grin on her face. You know the one."

"Yeah." And she could see it, perfectly. "I'm so happy for her, for you. It's like all that love was there, waiting, and the stones..." She looked down at them again. "They opened the door for it."

"And you, Grace? Have they opened the door for you?"

"I don't know if I'm ready for that." Nerves suddenly sprang to her fingertips. She laid the stone back in its bed. "Seth certainly wouldn't be. I don't think he'd believe in magic of any sort. And as for love... even if that door is wide open and the opportunity is there, he's not a man to fall easily."

"Easy or not—" Bailey closed the lid, replaced the box "—when you're meant to fall, you fall. He's yours, Grace. I saw that in your eyes this morning."

"Well." Grace swallowed the nerves. "I think I may wait awhile to let him in on that."

Chapter 8

There were flowers waiting for her when Grace returned to Cade's. A gorgeous crystal vase was filled with long spears of paper-white long-stemmed roses. Her heart thudded foolishly into her throat as she snatched up the card, tore open the envelope.

Then it deflated and sank.

Not from Seth, she noted. Of course, it had been silly of her to think that he'd have indulged in such a romantic and extravagant gesture. The card read simply:

Until we meet again,

Gregor

The ambassador with the oddly compelling eyes, she mused, and leaned forward to sniff at the tender, just-opening blooms. It had been sweet of him, she told herself. A bit over-the-top, as there were easily three dozen roses in the vase, but sweet.

And she was irritated to realize that if they had been from Seth, she would have mooned over them like a starstruck teenager, would likely have pressed one between the pages of a book, even shed a few tears. She berated herself for being six times a fool.

If these appalling highs and lows were side effects of being in love, Grace thought she could have waited quite a bit longer to experience the sensation. She was just about to toss the card on the table when the phone rang.

She hesitated, as both Cade's and Jack's cars were in the drive, but when the phone rang the third time, she picked it up. "Parris residence."

"Is Grace Fontaine available?" The crisp tones of a well-trained secretary sounded in her ear. "Ambassador DeVane calling."

"Yes, this is she."

"One moment, please, Ms. Fontaine."

Lips pursed thoughtfully, Grace flipped the edge of the card against her palm. The man certainly had had no trouble tracking her down, Grace mused. And just how was she going to handle him?

"Grace." His voice flowed through the phone. "How delightful to speak with you again."

"Gregor." She flipped her hair behind her shoulder, edged a hip onto the table. "How extravagant of you. I've just walked in to your roses." She tipped one down, sniffed again. "They're glorious."

"Merely a token. I was disappointed not to have more time with you last evening. You left so early."

She thought of the wild ride to Seth's, the wilder sex. "I had…a previous engagement."

"Perhaps we can make up for it tomorrow evening. I have a box at the theater. *Tosca.* It's such a beautiful tragedy. There's nothing I would enjoy more than sharing it with you, then a late supper, perhaps."

"It sounds lovely." She rolled her eyes toward the flowers. Oh, dear, she thought. This would never do. "I'm so terribly sorry, Gregor, but I'm not free." With no regret whatsoever, she set the card aside. "Actually, I'm involved with someone, quite seriously."

For me, in any case, she thought. Then she looked through the glass panels of the front door, and her face lit up with surprise and pleasure when she saw Seth's car pull in.

"I see." She was too busy trying to steady her abruptly dancing pulse to notice how his voice had chilled. "Your escort of last evening."

"Yes. I'm terribly flattered, Gregor, and if I were any less involved, I'd leap at the invitation. I hope you'll forgive me, and understand."

Struggling not to squirm with delight, she crooked her finger in invitation as Seth stepped up to the door.

"Of course. If your circumstances change, I hope you'll reconsider."

"I certainly will." With a sultry smile, she walked her fingers up Seth's chest. "And thank you again, Gregor, so much, for the flowers. They're divine."

"It was my pleasure," he said, and his hands balled into bone-white fists as he hung up the receiver.

Humiliated, he thought, snapping his teeth together, grinding them viciously. Rejected for a suitful of muscles and a badge.

She would pay, he promised himself, taking her photo from his file and gently tapping a well-manicured finger against it. She would pay dearly. And soon.

With the ambassador completely forgotten the moment the connection was broken, Grace tipped her face up to Seth's. "Hello, handsome."

He didn't kiss her, but looked at the flowers, then at the card she'd tossed carelessly beside them. "Another conquest?"

"Apparently." She heard the cold distance in his tone and wasn't certain whether to be flattered or annoyed. She opted for a different tack altogether, and purred. "The ambassador was interested in an evening at the opera and…whatever."

The spurt of jealousy infuriated him. It was a new experience, and one he detested. It left him helpless, made him want to drag her out to his car by the hair, cart her off, lock her up where only he could see and touch and taste.

But more, there was fear, for her. A bone-deep sense of danger.

"It seems the ambassador—and you—move quickly."

No, she realized, the temper was going to come. There was no stopping it. She eased off the table, her smile an icy dare. "I move however it suits me. You should know."

"Yes." He dipped his hands into his pockets to keep them off her. "I should. I do."

Crushed, she angled her chin, aimed those laser blue eyes. "Which am I now, Lieutenant? The whore or the goddess? The ivory princess atop the pedestal, or the tramp? I've been them all—it just depends on the man and how he chooses to look."

"I'm looking at you," he said calmly. "And I don't know what I see."

"Let me know when you make up your mind." She started to move around him, came up short when he took her arm. "Don't push me." She tossed her head so that her hair flew out, settled.

"I could say the same, Grace."

She drew in one hot, deep breath, shoved his hand

aside. "If you're interested, I gave the ambassador my regrets and told him I was involved with someone." She flashed a frigid smile and swung toward the stairs. "That, apparently, was my mistake."

He scowled after her, considered striding up the stairs of a house that wasn't his own and finishing the confrontation—one way or the other. Appalled, he pinched the bridge of his nose between his thumb and forefinger and tried to squeeze off the bitter headache plaguing him.

His day had been grueling, and had ended ten long hours after it began, with him staring at the group of photos on his board. Photos of the dead who were waiting for him to find the connection.

And he was already furious with himself because he'd already begun to run a search for data on Gregor DeVane. He couldn't be sure if he had done so due to a basic cop's hunch, or a man's territorial instinct. Or the dreams. It was a question, and a conflict, he'd never had to face before.

But one answer was clear as glass. He'd been out of line with Grace. He was still standing by the foyer table, frowning at the steps and weighing his options, when Cade strolled in from the rear of the house.

"Buchanan." More than a little surprised to see the homicide lieutenant standing in his foyer scowling,

Cade stopped, scratched his jaw. "Ah, I didn't know you were here."

He had no business being there, Seth reminded himself. "Sorry. Grace let me in."

"Oh." After one beat, Cade pinpointed the source of the heat still flashing in the air. "Oh," he said again, and wisely controlled a grin. "Fine. Something I can do for you?"

"No. I'm just leaving."

"Have a spat?"

Seth turned his head, met Cade's obviously amused eyes blandly. "Excuse me?"

"Just a wild stab in the dark. What did you do to tick her off?" Though Seth didn't answer, Cade noted that his gaze shifted briefly to the roses. "Oh, yeah. Guess you didn't send them, huh? If some guy sent Bailey three dozen white roses, I'd probably have to stuff them down his throat, one at a time."

It was the gleam of appreciation that flashed briefly in Seth's eyes that made Cade decide to revise his stance. Maybe he could like Lieutenant Seth Buchanan after all.

"Want a beer?"

The casual and friendly invitation threw Seth off balance. "I— No, I was leaving."

"Come on out back. Jack and I already popped a couple of tops. We're going to fire up the grill and show the women how real men cook." Cade's grin spread charmingly. "Besides, oiling yourself with a couple of brews will make it easier for you to crawl. You're going to crawl anyway, so you might as well be comfortable."

Seth hissed out a breath. "Why the hell not?"

Grace stayed stubbornly in her room for an hour. She could hear laughter, music, and the silly whack of mallets striking balls as people played an enthusiastic game of croquet. She knew Seth's car was still in the drive, and had promised herself she wouldn't go back down until it was gone.

But she was feeling deprived, and hungry.

Since she'd already changed into shorts and a thin cotton shirt, she paused at the mirror only long enough to freshen her lipstick, spritz on some perfume. Just to make him suffer, she told herself, then sauntered downstairs and out onto the patio.

Steaks were smoking on the grill with Cade at the helm wielding an enormous barbecue fork. Bailey and Jack were arguing over the croquet match, and M.J. was sulking at a picnic table while she nibbled on po-tato chips.

"Jack knocked me out of the game," she complained, and gestured with her beer. "I still say he cheated."

"Any time you lose," Grace pointed out as she picked

up a chip, "it's because someone cheated." Then she slid her gaze to Seth.

He'd taken off his tie, she noted, and his jacket. He still wore his holster. She imagined that was because he didn't feel comfortable hanging his gun over a tree branch. He, too, had a beer in his hand, and was watching the game with apparent interest.

"You still here?"

"Yeah." He'd had two beers, but didn't think crawling was going to be any more comfortable with the lubricant. "I've been invited to dinner."

"Isn't that cozy?" Grace spied what she recognized as a pitcher of M.J.'s special margaritas and poured herself a glass. The taste was tart, icy, and perfect. In dismissal, she wandered over to the grill to kibitz.

"I know what I'm doing," Cade was saying, and shifted to guard his territory as Seth joined them. "I marinated these vegetable kabobs personally. Go away and leave this to a man."

"I was merely asking if you preferred your mushrooms blackened."

Cade sent her a withering look. "Get her off my back, Seth. An artist can't work with critics breathing down his neck and picking on his mushrooms."

"Let's go over here." Seth took her elbow, and was braced for her jerk. He kept his grip firm and hauled her away into the rose garden.

"I don't want to talk to you," Grace said furiously.

"You don't have to talk. I'll talk." But it took him a minute. Apologies didn't come easily to a man who made it a habit not to make mistakes. "I'm sorry. I overreacted."

She said nothing, simply folded her arms and waited.

"You want more?" He nodded, didn't bother to sigh. "I was jealous, an atypical reaction for me, and I handled it poorly. I apologize."

Grace shook her head. "That's the weakest excuse for an apology I've ever heard. Not the words, Seth, the delivery. But fine, I'll accept it in the same spirit it was offered."

"What do you want from me?" he demanded, frustrated enough to raise his voice and grab her arms. "What the hell do you want?"

"That." She tossed back her head. "Just that. A little emotion, a little passion. You can take your cardboard-stiff apology and stuff it, just like you can stuff the cold, deliberate and dispassionate routine you gave me over the flowers. That icy control doesn't cut it with me. If you feel something—whatever the hell it is— then let me know."

She sucked in her breath, stunned, when he yanked her against him, savaged her mouth with heat and anger and need. She twisted once and was hauled roughly back. Then was left weak and singed and shaken by the time he drew away.

"Is that enough for you?" He hauled her to her toes, his fingers digging in. His eyes weren't dispassionate now, weren't cool, but turbulent. Human. "Enough emotion, enough passion? I don't like to lose control. You can't afford to lose control on the job."

Her breath was heaving. And her heart was flying. "This isn't the job."

"No, but it was supposed to be." He willed his grip to loosen. "You were supposed to be. I can't get you out of my head. Damn it, Grace. I can't get you out."

She laid a hand on his cheek, felt the muscle twitch. "It's the same for me. Maybe the only difference right now is that I want it to be that way."

For how long? he wondered, but he didn't say it. "Come home with me."

"I'd love to." She smiled, stroked her fingers back, into his hair. "But I think we'd better stay for dinner, at least. Otherwise, we'd break Cade's heart."

"After dinner, then." It wasn't difficult at all, he discovered, to bring her hands to his lips, linger over them, then look into her eyes. "I am sorry. But, Grace—?"

"Yes?"

"If DeVane calls you again, or sends flowers?"

Her lips twitched. "Yes?"

"I'll have to kill him."

With a delighted laugh, she threw her arms around Seth's neck. "Now we're talking."

"That was nice." With a satisfied sigh, Grace sank down in the seat of Seth's car and watched the moon shimmer in the sky. "I like seeing the four of them together. But it's funny. It's as if I blinked, and everyone took this huge, giant step forward."

"Red light, green light."

Confused, Grace turned her head to look at him. "What?"

"The game—the kid's game? You know, the person who's it has to say, 'Green light,' turn his back. Everybody can go forward, but then he says, 'Red light' and spins around. If he sees anybody move, they have to go back to the start."

When she gave a baffled laugh, it was his turn to look. "Didn't you ever play games like that when you were a kid?"

"No. I was given the proper lessons, lectured on etiquette and was instructed to take brisk daily walks for exercise. Sometimes I ran," she said softly, remembering. "Fast, and hard, until my heart was bumping in my chest. But I guess I always had to go back to the start."

Annoyed with herself, she shook her shoulders. "My, doesn't that sound pathetic? It wasn't, really. It was just structured." She scooped back her hair, smiled at him. "So what other games did young Seth Buchanan play?"

"The usual." Didn't she know how heartbreaking it was to hear that wistfulness in her voice, then see that quick, careless shrug as she pushed it all aside? "Didn't you have friends?"

"Of course." Then she looked away. "No. It doesn't matter. I have them now. The best of friends."

"Do you know any one of the three of you can start a sentence and either of the other two can finish it?"

"We don't do that."

"Yes, you do. A dozen times tonight, at least. You don't even realize it. And you have this code," he continued. "Little quirks and gestures. M.J.'s half smirk or eye roll, Bailey's downsweep of the lashes or hair-around-the-finger twist. And you lift your left brow, just a fraction, or catch your tongue between your teeth. When you do, you let each other know the joke's your little secret."

She hummed in her throat, not at all sure she liked being deciphered so easily. "Aren't you observant...."

"That's my job." He pulled into his driveway, turned to her. "It shouldn't bother you."

"I haven't decided if it does or not. Did you become a cop because you're observant, or are you observant because you're a cop?"

"Hard to say. I was never really anything else."

"Not even when you were young Seth Buchanan?"

"It was always part of my life. My grandfather was a cop. And my father. My father's brother. Our house was filled with them."

"So it was expected of you?"

"It was understood," he corrected. "If I'd wanted to be a plumber or a mechanic, that would have been fine. But it was what I wanted."

"Why?"

"There's right and there's wrong."

"Just that simple?"

"It should be." He looked at the ring on his finger. "My father was a good cop. Straight. Fair. Solid. You can't ask for more than that."

She laid a hand over his. "You lost him."

"Line of duty. A long time ago." The hurt had passed a long time before, as well, and left room for pride. "He was a good cop, a good father, a good man. He always said there was a choice between doing the right thing or the wrong thing. Either one had a price. But you could pay up on the first and still look yourself in the eye every morning."

Grace leaned over, kissed him lightly. "He did the right thing by you."

"Always. My mother was a cop's wife, steady as a rock. Now she's a cop's mother, and she's still steady.

Still there. When I got my gold shield, it meant as much to her as it did to me."

There was a bond, she realized. Deep and true and unquestioned. "But she worries about you."

"Some. But she accepts it. Has to," he added, with the ghost of a smile. "I've got a younger brother and sister. We're all cops."

"It runs through the blood," she murmured. "Are you close?"

"We're family," he said simply, then thought of hers and remembered that such things weren't simple. They were precious. "Yes, we're close."

He was the oldest, she mused. He would have taken his generational placement seriously, and, when his father died, his responsibilities as man of the house with equal weight.

It was hardly a wonder, then, that authority, responsibility, duty, sat so naturally on him. She thought of the weapon he wore, touched a fingertip to the leather strap.

"Have you ever…" She lifted her gaze to his. "Have you ever had to?"

"Yes. But I can still look myself in the eye in the morning."

She accepted that without question. But the next subject was more difficult. "You have a scar, just here."

Her memory of it was perfect as she touched her finger just under his right shoulder now. "You were shot?"

"Five years ago. One of those things." There was no point in relaying the details. The bust gone wrong, the shouts and the electric buzz of terror. The insult of the bullet and the bright, stupefying pain. "Most police work is routine—paperwork, tedium, repetition."

"But not all."

"No, not all." He wanted to see her smile again, wanted to prolong what had evolved into a sweet and intimate interlude in a darkened car. Just conversation, without the sizzle of sex. "You've got a tattoo on your incredibly perfect bottom."

She laughed then, and tossed her hair back. "I didn't think you'd noticed."

"I noticed. Why do you have a tattoo of a winged horse on your butt, Grace?"

"It was an impulse, one of those wild-girl things I dragged M.J. and Bailey into."

"They have winged horses on their—"

"No, and what they do have is their little secret. I wanted the winged horse because it was free. You couldn't catch it unless it wanted to be caught." She lifted a hand to his face, changed the mood subtly. "I never wanted to be caught. Before."

He nearly believed her. Lowering his head, he met

her lips with his, let the kiss spin out. It was quiet, without urgency. The slow meeting of tongues, the lazy change of angles and depths. Easy sips. Testing nibbles.

Her body shifted fluidly, her hands sliding up his chest to link at the nape of his neck. A purr sounded in her throat. "It's been a long time since I necked in the front seat of a car."

He nudged her hair aside so that his mouth could find that sweet, sensitive curve between neck and shoulder. "Want to try the back seat?"

Her laugh was low and delighted. "Absolutely."

The need had snuck up on him, crept into his bloodstream to stagger his heart. "We'll go inside."

Her breath was a bit unsteady as she leaned back, grinned at him in the shimmer of moonlight. "Chicken."

His eyes narrowed fractionally, making her grin widen. "There's a perfectly good bed in the house."

She made a soft clucking noise, then, chuckling, rubbed her lips over his. "Let's pretend," she whispered, pressing her body to his, sliding it against his. "We're on a dark, deserted road and you've told me the car's broken down."

He said her name, an exasperated sound against her tempting lips. It was only another challenge to her.

"I pretend I believe you, because I want to stay, I want you to...persuade me. You'll say you just want to touch me, and I'll pretend I believe that, too." She took his hand, laid it on her breast and felt the quick thrill when his fingers flexed. "Even though I know that's not all you want. It's not all you want, is it, Seth?"

What he wanted was that dark, slippery slide into her. His hands moved under her shirt, found flesh. "We're not going to make it into the back seat," he warned her.

She only laughed.

He wasn't sure if he felt smug or stunned by his own behavior when he finally unlocked his front door. Had he been this randy as a teenager? he wondered. That ridiculously reckless. Or was it only Grace who made such things as making desperate love in his own drive-way one more adventure?

She stepped inside, lifted the hair off her neck, then let it fall in a gesture that simply stopped his heart. "My place should be ready by tomorrow, the next day at the latest. We'll have to go there. We can skinny-dip in my pool. It's so hot out now."

"You're so beautiful."

She turned, surprised at the mix of resentment and desire in his voice. He stood just inside the door, as if he might turn at any moment and leave her.

"It's a dangerous weapon. Lethal."

She tried to smile. "Arrest me."

"You don't like to be told." He let out a half laugh. "You don't like to be told you're beautiful."

"I didn't do anything to earn how I look."

She said it, he realized, as if beauty were more of a curse than a gift. And in that moment he felt a new level of understanding. He stepped forward, took her face gently in his hands, looked deep and long.

"Well, maybe your eyes are a little too close together."

Her hitch of laughter was pure surprise. "They are not."

"And your mouth, I think it might be just a hair off center. Let me check." He measured it with his own, lingering over the kiss when her lips curved. "Yeah. Just a hair, but it does throw things off, now that I really look. And let's see…" He turned her head to each side, paused to consider. "Yep. The left profile's weak. Are you getting a double chin there?"

She slapped his hand away, torn between insult and laughter. "I certainly am not."

"I really should check that, too. I don't know if I want to take this whole thing any further if you're getting a double chin."

He grabbed her, tugging her head back gently by the hair so that he could nibble freely under her jaw. She giggled—a young, foolish sound—and squirmed.

"Stop that, you idiot." She let out a shriek when he hauled her up into his arms.

"You're no lightweight, either, by the way."

Her eyes went to slits. "Okay, buster, that's all. I'm leaving."

It was a delight to watch him grin—that quick, boyish flash of humor. "I forgot to tell you," he said as he headed for the stairs. "My car's broken down. I'm out of gas. The cat ate my homework. I'm just going to touch you."

He'd made it up two steps when the phone rang. "Damn." He brushed his lips absently over her brow. "I have to get that."

"It's all right. I'll remember where you were." Though he set her down, she didn't think her feet hit the floor. Love was a cushy buffer.

But her smile faded as she saw his eyes change. Suddenly they were flat again, unreadable. She knew as she walked across the room toward him that he'd shifted seamlessly from man to cop.

"Where?" His voice was cool again, controlled. "Is the scene secured?" He swore lightly, barely a whisper under the breath. "Get it secured. I'm on my way." As he hung up, his eyes skimmed over her, focused. "I'm sorry, Grace, I have to go."

She moistened her lips. "Is it bad?"

"I have to go," was all he'd say. "I'll call for a black-and-white to take you back to Cade's."

"Can't I wait here for you?"

"I don't know how long I'll be."

"It doesn't matter." She offered a hand, but wasn't sure she could reach him. "I'd like to wait. I want to wait for you."

No woman ever had. That thought passed quickly through his mind, distracting him. "If you get tired of waiting, call the precinct. I'll leave word there for a uniform to drive you home if you call in."

"All right." But she wouldn't call in. She would wait. "Seth." She moved into him, brushed her lips against his. "I'll see you when you get back."

Chapter 9

Alone, Grace switched on the television, settled on the sofa. Five minutes later, she was up and wandering the house.

He didn't go in for knickknacks, she mused. Probably thought of them as dustcatchers. No plants, no pets. The living room furniture was simple, masculine, and good quality. The sofa was comfortable, of generous size and a deep hunter green. She would have spruced it up with pillows. Burgundy, navy, copper. The coffee table was a square of heavy oak, highly polished and dust-free.

She decided he had a weekly housekeeper. She just couldn't picture Seth wielding a polishing rag. There was a bookcase under the side window and, crouching, she scanned the titles. It pleased her that they had read many of the same books. There was even a gardening book she'd studied herself.

That she could see, she decided. Yes, she could see Seth working out in the yard, turning the earth, planting something that would last.

There was art in this room, as well. She moved closer, certain the watercolor portraits grouped on the wall were the work of the same artist who had done the cityscape and rural scene in his bedroom. She searched for the signature first, and found Marilyn Buchanan looped in the lower corner.

Sister, mother, cousin? she wondered. Someone he loved, and who loved him. She shifted her gaze and studied the first painting.

Seth's father, Grace realized with a jolt. It had to be. The resemblance was there, in the eyes, clear, intense, tawny. The jaw, squared off, almost chiseled. The artist had seen strength, a touch of sadness, and honor. A whisper of humor around the mouth and an innate pride in the set of the head. All were evident in the three-quarter profile view that had the subject staring off at something only he could see.

The next portrait was a woman, perhaps in her forties. It was a pretty face, but the artist hadn't hidden the faint and telltale lines of age, the touches of gray in the dark, curling hair. The hazel eyes looked straight ahead, with humor and with patience. And there was Seth's mouth, Grace thought, smiling easily.

His mother, she concluded. How much strength was contained inside those quiet gray eyes? Grace wondered. How much was required to stand and accept when everyone you loved faced danger daily?

Whatever the amount, this woman possessed it.

There was another man, young, twenty-something, with a cocky grin and daredevil eyes shades darker than Seth's. Attractive, sexy, with a dark shock of hair falling carelessly over his brow. His brother, certainly.

The last was of a young woman with a shoulder-length sweep of dark hair, the tawny eyes alert, the sculpted mouth just curved in the beginnings of a smile. Lovely, with more of Seth's seriousness about her than the young man. His sister.

She wondered if she would ever meet them, or if she would know them only through their portraits. Seth would take the woman he loved to them, she thought, and let the little slice of hurt pass through her. He would want to—need to—bring her into his mother's home, watch how she melded and mixed with his family.

It was a door he'd have to open on both sides in welcome. Not just because it was traditional, she realized, but because it would matter to him.

But a lover? No, she decided. It wasn't necessary to

share a lover with family. He'd never take a woman with whom he shared only sex home to meet his mother.

Grace closed her eyes a moment. Stop feeling sorry for yourself, she ordered briskly. You can't have everything you want or need, so you make the best of what there is.

She opened her eyes again, once more scanned the portraits. Good faces, she thought. A good family.

But where, Grace wondered, was Seth's portrait? There had to be one. What had the artist seen? Had she painted him with that cool cop's stare, that surprisingly beautiful smile, the all-too-rare flash of that grin?

Determined to find out, she left the television blaring and went on the hunt. In the next twenty minutes, she discovered that Seth lived tidily, kept a phone and notepad in every room, used the second bedroom as a combination guest room and office, had turned the tiny third bedroom into a minigym and liked deep colors and comfortable chairs.

She found more watercolors, but no portrait of the man.

She circled the guest room, curious that here, and only here, he'd indulged in some whimsy. Recessed shelves held a collection of figures, some carved in wood, others in stone. Dragons, griffins, sorcerers, unicorns, centaurs. And a single winged horse of alabaster caught soaring in midflight.

Here the paintings reflected the magical—a misty landscape where a turreted castle rose silver into a pale rose-colored sky, a shadow-dappled lake where a single white deer drank.

There were books on Arthur, on Irish legends, the gods of Olympus, and those who had ruled Rome. And there, on the small cherrywood desk, was a globe of blue crystal and a book on Mithra, the god of light.

It made her tremble, clutch her arms. Had he picked up the book because of the case? Or had it already been here? She touched a hand to the slim volume and was certain it was the latter.

One more link between them, she realized, forged before they'd even met. It was so easy for her to accept that, even to be grateful. But she wondered if he felt the same.

She went downstairs, oddly at home after her self-guided tour. It made her smile to see their coffee cups from that morning still in the sink, a little touch of intimacy. She found a bottle of wine in the refrigerator, poured herself a glass and took it with her into the living room.

She went back to the bookcase, thinking of curling up on the couch with the TV for company and a book to pass the time. Then a chill washed over her, so quick, so intense, the wine shook in her hand. She found herself staring out the window, her breath coming short, her other hand clutched on the edge of the bookcase.

Someone watching. It pounded in her brain, a frightened, whispering voice that might have been her own.

Someone watching.

But she saw nothing but the dark, the shimmer of moonlight, the quiet house across the street.

Stop it, she ordered herself. There's no one there. There's nothing there. But she straightened and quickly twitched the curtains closed. Her hands were shaking.

She sipped wine, tried to laugh at herself. The late-breaking bulletin on the television had her turning slowly. A family of four in nearby Bethesda. Murdered.

She knew where Seth had gone now. And could only imagine what he was dealing with.

She was alone. DeVane sat in his treasure room, stroking an ivory statue of the goddess Venus. He'd come to think of it as Grace. As his obsession festered and grew, he imagined Grace and himself together, immortal through time. She would be his most prized possession. His goddess. And the Three Stars would complete his collection of the priceless.

Of course, she would have to be punished first. He knew what had to be done, what would matter most to her. And the other two women were not blameless—

they had complicated his plans, caused him to fail. They would have to die, of course.

After he had the Stars, after he had Grace, they would die. And their deaths would be her punishment.

Now she was alone. It would be so easy to take her now. To bring her here. She'd be afraid, at first. He wanted her to be afraid. It was part of her punishment. Eventually he would woo her, win her. Own her. They would have, after all, several lifetimes to be together.

In one of them he would take her back to Terresa. He would make her a queen. A god could settle for no less than a queen.

Take her tonight. The voice that spoke louder and louder in his head every day taunted him. He couldn't trust it. DeVane steadied his breathing, shut his eyes. He would not be rushed. Every detail had to be in place.

Grace would come to him when he was prepared. And she would bring him the Stars.

Seth downed one last cup of sludgy coffee and rubbed at the ache at the back of his neck. His stomach was still raw from what he'd seen in that neat suburban home. He knew civilians and rookie cops believed the vets became immune to the results of violent death—the sights, the smells, the meaningless waste.

It was a lie.

No one could become used to seeing what he'd seen. If they could, they shouldn't wear a badge. The law needed to retain its sense of disgust, of horror, for murder.

What drove a man to take the lives of his own children, of the woman he'd made them with, and then his own? There'd been no one left in that neat suburban home to answer that question. He knew it would haunt him.

Seth scrubbed his hands over his face, felt the knots of tension and fatigue. He rolled his shoulders once, twice, then squared them before cutting through the bull pen, toward the locker room.

Mick Marshall was there, rubbing his sore feet. His wiry red hair stood up like a bush that needed trimming from a face lined with weariness. His eyes were shadowed, his mouth was grim.

"Lieutenant." He pulled his socks back on.

"You didn't have to come in on this, Detective."

"Hell, I heard the gunshots from my own living room." He picked up one of his shoes, but just rested his elbows on his knees. "Two blocks over. Jesus, my kids played with those kids. How the hell am I going to explain this?"

"How well did you know the father?"

"Didn't, really. It's just like they always say, Lieu-

tenant. He was a quiet guy, polite, kept to himself."
He gave a short, humorless laugh. "They always do."

"Mulrooney's taking the case. You can assist if you
want. Now go home, get some sleep. Go in and kiss
your kids."

"Yeah." Mick scraped his fingers through his hair.
"Listen, Lieutenant, I got some data on that DeVane
guy."

Seth's spine tingled. "Anything interesting?"

"Depends on what floats your boat. He's fifty-two,
never married, inherited a big fat pile from his old man,
including this big vineyard on that island, that Terresa.
Grows olives, too, runs some cattle."

"The gentleman farmer?"

"Oh, he's got more going than that. Lots of interests,
spread out all over hell and back. Shipping, communi-
cations, import-export. Lots of fingers in lots of pies
generating lots of dough. He was made ambassador
to the U.S. three years ago. Seems to like it here. He
bought some nifty place on Foxhall Road, big man-
sion, likes to entertain. People don't like to talk about
him, though. They get real nervous."

"Money and power make some people nervous."

"Yeah. I haven't gotten a lot of information yet. But
there was a woman about five years ago. Opera singer.
Pretty big deal, if you're into that sort of thing. Ital-

ian lady. Seems like they were pretty tight. Then she disappeared."

"Disappeared." Seth's waning interest snapped back. "How?"

"That's the thing. She just went poof. Italian police can't figure it. She had a place in Milan, left all her things—clothes, jewelry, the works. She was singing at that opera house there, in the middle of a run, you know? Didn't show for the evening performance. She went shopping on that afternoon, had a bunch of things sent back to her place. But she never went back."

"They figure kidnapping?"

"They did. But then there was no ransom call, no body, no sign of her in nearly five years. She was…" Mick screwed up his face in thought. "Thirty, supposed to be at the top of her form, and a hell of a looker. She left a big pile of lire in her accounts. It's still there."

"DeVane was questioned?"

"Yeah. Seems he was on his yacht in the Ionian Sea, soaking up rays and drinking ouzo, when it all went down. A half-dozen guests on board with him. The Italian cop I talked to—big opera fan, by the way—he didn't think DeVane seemed shocked enough, or upset enough. He smelled something, but couldn't make anything stick. Still, the guy offered a reward, five million lire, for her safe return. No one ever collected."

"I'd say that was fairly interesting. Keep digging."

And, Seth thought, he'd start doing some digging himself.

"One more thing." Mick cracked his neck from side to side. "And I thought this was interesting too—the guy's a collector. He has a little of everything—coins, stamps, jewelry, art, antiques, statuary. He does it all. But he's also reputed to have a unique and extensive gem collection—rivals the Smithsonian's."

"DeVane likes rocks."

"Oh, yeah. And get this. Two years ago, more or less, he paid three mil for an emerald. Big rock, sure, but its price spiked because it was supposed to be a magic rock." The very idea made Mick's lips curl. "Merlin was supposed to have, you know, conjured it up for Arthur. Seems to me a guy who'd buy into that would be pretty interested in three big blue rocks and all that god and immortality stuff that goes with them."

"I just bet he would." And wasn't it odd, Seth mused, that DeVane's name hadn't been on Bailey's list? A collector whose U.S. residence was only miles from Salvini, yet he'd never done business with them?

No, the lack was too odd to believe.

"Get me what you've got when you go on shift, Mick. I'd like to talk to that Italian cop personally. I appreciate the extra time you put into this."

Mick blinked. Seth never failed to thank his men for good work, but it was generally mechanical. There had been genuine warmth this time, on a personal level. "Sure, no sweat. But you know, Lieutenant, even if you can tie this guy to the case, he'll bounce. Diplomatic immunity. We can't touch him."

"Let's tie him first, then we'll see." Seth glanced over, distracted, when a locker slammed open nearby as a cop was coming on shift. "Get some sleep," he began, then broke off. There, taped to the back of the locker, was Grace, young, laughing and naked.

Her head was tossed back, and that teasing smile, that feminine confidence, that silky power, sparkled in her eyes. Her skin was like polished marble, her curves were generous, with only that rainfall of hair, artfully draped to drive a man insane, covering her.

Mick turned his head, saw the centerfold and winced. Cade had filled him in on the lieutenant's relationship with Grace, and all Mick could think was that someone—very likely the cop currently standing at his locker whistling moronically—was about to die.

"Ah, Lieutenant…" Mick began, with some brave thought of saving his associate's life.

Seth merely held up a hand, cut Mick off and walked to the locker. The cop changing his shirt glanced over. "Lieutenant."

"Bradley," Seth said, and continued to study the glossy photo.

"She's something else, isn't she? One of the guys on

day shift said she'd been in and looked just as good in person."

"Did he?"

"You bet. I dug this out of a pile of magazines in my garage. None the worse for wear."

"Bradley." Mick whispered the name and buried his head in his hands. The guy was dead meat.

Seth took a long breath, resisted the urge to rip the photo down. "Female officers share this locker room, Bradley. This is inappropriate." Where was the tattoo? Seth thought hazily. What had she been when she posed for this? Nineteen, twenty? "Find somewhere else to hang your art."

"Yes, sir."

Seth turned away, then shot one last look over his shoulder. "And she's better in person. Much better."

"Bradley," Mick said as Seth strode out, "you just dodged one major bullet."

Dawn was breaking when Seth let himself into the house. He'd gone by the book on the case in Bethesda. It would close when the forensic and autopsy reports confirmed what he already knew. A man of thirty-six who made a comfortable living as a computer programmer had gotten up from his sofa, where he was watching television, loaded his revolver and ended four lives in the approximate space of ten minutes.

For this crime, Seth could offer no justice.

He could have headed home two hours earlier. But he'd made use of the time difference in Europe to make calls, ask questions, gather data. He was slowly putting together a picture of Gregor DeVane.

A man of wealth he had never sweated for. One who enjoyed prestige and power, who traveled in exalted circles, and had no family.

There was no crime in any of that, Seth thought as he closed his front door behind him.

There was no crime in sending white roses to a beautiful woman.

Or in once being involved with one who'd disappeared. But wasn't it interesting that DeVane had been involved with another woman? A Frenchwoman, a prima ballerina of great beauty who'd been considered the finest dancer of the decade. And who had been found dead of a drug overdose in her Paris home.

The verdict had been suicide, though those closest to her insisted she had never used drugs. She had been fiercely disciplined about her body. DeVane had been questioned in that matter, as well, but only as a matter of form. He had been dining at the White House at the very hour the young dancer slipped into a coma, and then into death.

Still, Seth and the Italian detective agreed it was quite a fascinating coincidence.

A collector, Seth mused, switching off lights automatically. An acquirer of beautiful things, and beautiful women. A man who would pay double the value of an emerald to possess a legend, as well.

He would see how many more threads he could tie, and he would, he decided, have an official chat with the ambassador.

He stepped into the living room, started to hit the next switch, and saw Grace curled upon the couch.

He'd assumed she'd gone home. But there she was, curled into a tight, protective ball on his couch, sleeping. What the hell was she doing here? he wondered.

Waiting for you. Just as she said she would. As no woman had waited before. As he'd wanted no woman to wait.

Emotion thudded into his chest, flooded into his heart. It undid him, he realized, this irrational love. His heart wasn't safe here, wasn't even his own any longer. He wanted it back, wanted desperately to be able to turn away, leave her and go back to his life.

It terrified him that he wouldn't. Couldn't.

She was bound to get bored before too much longer, to lose interest in a relationship he imagined was fueled by impulse and sex on her part. Would she just drift away, he wondered, or end it cleanly? It would be clean, he decided. That would be her way. She wasn't, as he'd once wanted to believe, callous or cold or calculating. She had a very giving heart, but he thought it was also a restless one.

Moving over, he crouched in front of her, studied her face. There was a faint line between her brows. She didn't sleep easily, he realized. What dreams chased her? he asked himself. What worries nagged her?

Poor little rich girl, he thought. Still running until you're out of breath and there's nothing to do but go back to the start.

He stroked a thumb over her brow to smooth it, then slid his arms under her. "Come on, baby," he murmured, "time for bed."

"No." She pushed at him, struggled. "Don't."

More nightmares? Concerned, he gathered her close. "It's Seth. It's all right. I've got you."

"Watching me." She turned her face into his shoulder. "Outside. Everywhere. Watching me."

"Shhh... No one's here." He carried her toward the steps, realizing now why every light in the house had been blazing. She'd been afraid to be alone in the dark. Yet she'd stayed. "No one's going to hurt you, Grace. I promise."

"Seth." She surfaced to the sound of his voice, and her heavy eyes opened and focused on his face. "Seth," she said again. She touched a hand to his cheek, then her lips. "You look so tired."

"We can switch. You can carry me."

She slid her arms around him, pressed her cheek, warm to his. "I heard, on the news. The family in Bethesda."

"You didn't have to wait."

"Seth." She eased back, met his eyes.

"I won't talk about it," he said flatly. "Don't ask."

"You won't talk about it because it troubles you to talk about it, or because you won't share those troubles with me?"

He set her down beside the bed, turned away and peeled off his shirt. "I'm tired, Grace. I have to be back in a few hours. I need to sleep."

"All right." She rubbed the heel of her hand over her heart, where it hurt the most. "I've already had some sleep. I'll go downstairs and call a cab."

He hung his shirt over the back of a chair, sat to take off his shoes. "If that's what you want."

"It's not what I want, but it seems it's what you want." She barely lifted a brow when he heaved his shoe across the room. Then he stared at it as if it had leaped there on its own.

"I don't do things like that," he said between his teeth. "I never do things like that."

"Why not? It always makes me feel better." And because he looked so exhausted, and so baffled by himself, she relented. Walking to him, she stepped in close to where he sat and began to knead the stiff muscles of his shoulders. "You know what you need around here, Lieutenant?" She dipped her head to kiss the top of his. "Besides me, of course. You need to get yourself a bubble tub, something you can sink down into that'll beat all these knots out of you. But for now we'll see what I can do about them."

Her hands felt like glory, smoothing out the knotted muscles in his shoulders. "Why?"

"That's one of your favorite questions, isn't it? Come on, lie down, let me work on this rock you call a back."

"I just need to sleep."

"Um-hmm." Taking charge, she nudged him back, climbed onto the bed to kneel beside him. "Roll over, handsome."

"I like this view better." He managed a half smile, toyed with the ends of her hair. "Why don't you come here? I'm too tired to fight you off."

"I'll keep that in mind." She gave him a push. "Roll over, big boy."

With a grunt, he rolled over on his stomach, then let out a second grunt when she straddled him and those wonderful hands began to press and stroke and knead.

"You, being you, would consider a regular massage an indulgence. But that's where you're wrong." She pressed down with the heels of her hands, worked forward to knead with her fingertips. "You give your body relief, it works better for you. I get one every week at the club. Stefan could do wonders for you."

"Stefan." He closed his eyes and tried not to think about another man with his hands all over her. "Figures."

"He's a professional," she said dryly. "And his wife is a pediatric therapist. She's wonderful with the children at the hospital."

He thought of the children, and that was what weakened him. That, and her soothing hands, her quiet voice. Sunlight filtered, a warm red, through his closed lids, but he could still see.

"The kids were in bed."

Her hands froze for a moment. Then, with a long, quiet breath, she moved them again, up and down his spine, over his shoulder blades, up to the tight length of his neck. And she waited.

"The youngest girl had a doll—one of those Raggedy Anns. An old one. She was still holding it. There were Disney posters all over the walls. All those fairy tales and happy endings. The way it's supposed to be when you're a kid. The older girl had one of those teen magazines beside the bed—the kind ten-year-olds read because they can't wait to be sixteen. They never woke up. Never knew neither one of them would get to be sixteen."

She said nothing. There was nothing that could

be said. But, leaning down, she touched her lips to the back of his shoulder and felt him let loose a long, ragged breath.

"It twists you when it's kids. I don't know a cop who can deal with it without having it twist his guts. The mother was on the stairs. Looks like she heard the shots, starting running up to her kids. After, he went back to the living room, sat down on the sofa and finished it."

She curled herself into him, hugged herself to his back and just held on. "Try to sleep," she murmured.

"Stay. Please."

"I will." She closed her eyes, listened to his breathing deepen. "I'll stay."

But he woke alone. As sleep was clearing, he wondered if he'd dreamed the meeting at dawn. Yet he could smell her—on the air, on his own skin where she'd curled close. He was still stretched crosswise over the bed, and he tilted his wrist to check the watch he'd neglected to take off.

Whatever else was going on inside him, his internal clock was still in working order.

He gave himself an extra two minutes under the shower to beat back fatigue, and when shaving promised himself to do nothing more than vegetate on his next personal day. He pretended it wasn't going to be another hot, humid, hazy day while he knotted his tie.

Then he swore, scooped fingers though his just-combed hair, remembering he'd neglected to set the timer on his coffeemaker. The minutes it would take to brew it would not only set his teeth on edge, they would eat into his schedule.

But the one thing he categorically refused to do was start the day with the poison that simmered at the cop shop.

His mind was so focused on coffee that when the scent of it wafted like a siren's call as he came down the stairs, he thought it was an illusion.

Not only was the pot full of gloriously rich black liquid, Grace was sitting at his kitchen table, reading the morning paper and nibbling on a bagel. Her hair was scooped back from her face, and she appeared to be wearing nothing more than one of his shirts.

"Good morning." She smiled up at him, then shook her head. "Are you human? How can you look so official and intimidating on less than three hours' sleep?"

"Practice. I thought you'd gone."

"I told you I'd stay. Coffee's hot. I hope you don't mind that I helped myself."

"No." He stood exactly where he was. "I don't mind."

"If it's all right with you, I'll just loiter over coffee awhile before I get dressed. I'll get myself back to

Cade's and change. I want to drop by the hospital later this morning, then I'm going home. It's time I did. The cleaning crew should be finished by this afternoon, so I thought…" She trailed off as he just continued to stare at her.

"What is it?" She gave an uncertain smile and rubbed at her nose.

Keeping his eyes on hers, he took the phone from the wall and punched in a number on memory. "This is Buchanan," he said. "I won't be in for a couple hours. I'm taking personal time." He hung up, held out a hand. "Come back to bed. Please."

She rose, and put her hand in his.

When clothes were scattered carelessly on the floor, the sheets turned back, the shades pulled to filter the beat of the sun, he covered her.

He needed to hold, to touch, to indulge himself for one hour with the flow of emotion she caused in him. Only an hour, yet he didn't hurry. Instead, he lingered over slow, deep, drugging kisses that lasted eons, loitered over long, smooth, soft caresses that stretched into forever.

She was there for him. Simply there. Open, giving, offering a seemingly endless supply of warmth.

She sighed, shakily, as he stroked her to helpless response, moving over her tenderly, his patience infinite. Each time their mouths met, with that slow slide of tongue, her heart shuddered in her breast.

There were the soft, slippery sounds of intimacy, the quiet murmurs of lovers, drifting into sighs and moans. Both of them were lost, mired in thick layers of sensation, the air around them like syrup, causing movement to slow and pleasure to last.

Her breath sighed out as he trailed lazily down her body with hands and mouth, as her own hands stroked over his back, then his shoulders. She opened for him, arching up in welcome, then shuddering as his tongue brought on a long, rolling climax.

And because he needed it as much as she, she let her hands fall limply, let him take her wherever he chose. Her blood beat hot and the heat brought a dew of roused passion to her skin. His hands slicked over her skin like silk.

"Tell me you want me." He trailed slow, open-mouthed kisses up her torso.

"Yes." She gripped his hips, urged him. "I want you."

"Tell me you need me." His tongue slid over her nipple.

"Yes." She moaned again when he suckled gently. "I need you."

Tell me you love me. But that he demanded only in his mind as he brought his mouth to hers again, sank into that wet, willing promise.

"Now." He kept his eyes open and on hers.

"Yes." She rose to meet him. "Now."

He glided inside her, filling her so slowly, so achingly, that they both trembled. He saw her eyes swim with tears and found the urge for tenderness stronger than any other. He kissed her again, softly, moved inside her one slow beat at a time.

The sweetness of it had a tear spilling over, trailing down her glowing cheek. Her lips trembled, and he felt her muscles contract and clutch him. "Don't close your eyes." He whispered it, sipped the tear from her cheek. "I want to see your eyes when I take you over."

She couldn't stop it. The tenderness stripped her. Her vision blurred with tears, and the blue of her eyes deepened to midnight. She said his name, then murmured it again against his lips. And her body quivered as the next long, undulating wave swamped her.

"I can't—"

"Let me have you." He was falling, falling, falling, and he buried his face in her hair. "Let me have all of you."

Chapter 10

In the nursery, Grace was rocking an infant. The baby girl was barely big enough to fill the crook of her arm from elbow to wrist, but the tiny infant watched her steadily with the deeply blue eyes of a newborn.

The hole in her heart had been repaired, and her prognosis was good.

"You're going to be fine, Carrie. Your mama and papa are so worried about you, but you're going to be just fine. She stroked the baby's cheek and thought—hoped—Carrie smiled a little.

Grace was tempted to sing her to sleep, but knew the nursing staff rolled their eyes and snickered whenever she tried a lullaby. Still, the babies were rarely critical of her admittedly poor singing voice, so she half sang, half murmured, until Carrie's baby owl's eyes grew heavy.

Even when she slept, Grace continued to rock. It was self-serving now, she knew. Anyone who had ever rocked a baby understood that it soothed the adult, as well as the child. And here, with an infant dozing in her arms, and her own eyes heavy, she could admit her deepest secret.

She pined for children of her own. She longed to carry them inside her, to feel the weight, the movement within, to push them into life with that last sharp pang of childbirth, to hold them to her breast and feel them drink from her.

She wanted to walk the floor with them when they were fretful, to watch them sleep. To raise them and watch them grow, she thought, closing her eyes as she rocked. To care for them, to comfort them in the night, even to watch them take that first wrenching step away from her.

Motherhood was her greatest wish and her most secret desire.

When she first involved herself with the pediatric wing, she'd worried that she was doing so to assuage that gnawing ache inside her. But she knew it wasn't true. The first time she held a sick child in her arms and gave comfort, she'd understood that her commitment encompassed so much more.

She had so much to give, such an abundance of love that needed to be offered. And here it could be accepted without question, without judgment. Here, at least, she could do something worthwhile, something that mattered.

"Carrie matters," she murmured, kissing the top of the sleeping baby's head before she rose to settle her in her crib. "And one day soon you'll go home, strong and healthy. You won't remember that I once rocked you to sleep when your mama couldn't be here. But I will."

She smiled at the nurse who came in, stepped back. "She seems so much better."

"She's a tough little fighter. You've got a wonderful touch with the babies, Ms. Fontaine." The nurse picked up charts, began to make notes.

"I'll try to give you an hour or so in a couple of days. And you'll be able to reach me at home again, if you need to."

"Oh?" The nurse looked up, peered over the top of wire-framed glasses. The murder at Grace's home, and the ensuing investigation, were hot topics at the hospital. "Are you sure you'll be…comfortable at home?"

"I'm going to make sure I'm comfortable." Grace gave Carrie a final look, then stepped out into the hall.

She just had time, she decided, to stop by the pediatric ward and visit the older children. Then she could call Seth's office and see if he was interested in a little dinner for two at her place.

She turned and nearly walked into DeVane.

"Gregor?" She fixed a smile on her face to mask the sudden odd bumping of her heart. "What a surprise. Is someone ill?"

He stared at her, unblinking. "Ill?"

What was wrong with his eyes? she wondered, that they seemed so pale and unfocused. "We are in the hospital," she said, keeping the smile on her face, and, vaguely concerned, she laid a hand on his arm. "Are you all right?"

He snapped back, appalled. For a moment, his mind seemed to have switched off. He'd only been able to see her, to smell her. "Quite well," he assured her. "Momentarily distracted. I didn't expect to see you, either."

Of course, that was a lie, he'd planned the meeting meticulously. He took her hand, bowed over it, kissed her fingers.

"It is, of course, a pleasure to see you anywhere. I've come by here as our mutual friends interested me in the care children receive here. Children and their welfare are a particular interest of mine."

"Really?" Her smile warmed immediately. "Mine, too. Would you like a quick tour?"

"With you as my guide, how could I not?" He turned, signaled to two men who stood stiffly several paces back. "Bodyguards," he told Grace, tucking her hand into the crook of his arm and patting it. "Distressingly necessary in today's climate. Tell me, why am I so fortunate as to find you here today?"

As she usually did, she covered the truth and kept her privacy. "The Fontaines donated significantly to this particular wing. I like to stop in from time to time to see what the hospital's doing with it." She flashed a twinkling look. "And you just never know when you might run into a handsome doctor—or ambassador."

She strolled along, explaining various sections and wondering how much she might, with a little time and charm, wheedle out of him for the children. "General pediatrics is on the floor above. Since this section houses maternity, they wouldn't want kids zooming down the corridors while mothers are in labor or resting."

"Yes, children can be quite boisterous." He detested them. "It's one of my deepest regrets that I have none of my own. But having never found the right woman…" He gestured with his free hand. "As I grow older, I'm resigned to having no one to carry on my name."

"Gregor, you're in your prime. A strong, vital man who can have as many children as he likes for years yet."

"Ah." He looked into her eyes again. "But there is still the right woman to be found."

She felt a shiver of discomfort at his pointed statement and intense gaze. "I'm sure you'll find her. We have some preemies here." She stepped closer to the glass. "So tiny," she said softly. "So defenseless."

"It's a pity when they're flawed."

She frowned at his choice of words. "Some of them need more time under controlled conditions and medical care to fully develop. But I wouldn't call them flawed."

Another error, he thought with an inner sense of irritation. He could not seem to keep his mind sharp with her scent invading his senses. "Ah, my English is sometimes awkward. You must forgive me."

She smiled again, wanting to ease his obvious discomfort. "Your English is wonderful."

"Is it clever enough to convince you to share a quiet lunch with me? As friends," he said, lacing his smile with regret. "With similar interests."

She glanced, as he did, at the babies. It was tempting, she admitted. He was a charming man—a wealthy and influential one. She might, with careful campaigning, persuade him to assist her in setting up an international branch of Falling Star, an ambition that had been growing in her lately.

"I would love to, Gregor, but right now I'm simply swamped. I was just on my way home when I ran into you. I have to check on some…repairs." That seemed the simplest way to explain it. "But I'd love to have a rain check. One I'd hope to cash in very soon. There's something concerning our similar interestss that I'd love to have your advice on, and your input."

"I would love to be of any service whatsoever." He kissed her hand again. Tonight, he thought. He would have her tonight, and there would be no more need for this charade.

"That's so kind of you." Because she felt guilty for her disinterest and coolness in the face of his interest, she kissed his cheek. "I really must run. Do call me about that rain check. Next week, perhaps, for lunch." With a final, flashing smile, she dashed off.

As he watched her, his fisted fingers dug crescents into his palms. Fighting for control, he nodded to one of the silent men who waited for him. "Follow her only," he ordered. "And wait for instructions."

Cade didn't think of himself as a whiner—and, considering how well he tolerated his own family, he believed himself one of the most patient, most amiable, of men. But he was certain that if Grace had him shift one more piece of furniture from one end of her enormous living area to the other, he would break down and weep.

"It looks great."

"Hmm…" She stood, one hand on her hip, the fingers of the other tapping against her lip.

The gleam in her eye was enough to strike terror in Cade's heart and had his already aching muscles crying out in protest. "Really, fabulous. A hundred percent. Get the camera. I see a cover of *House and Garden* here."

"You're wheedling, Cade," she said absently. "Maybe the conversation pit did look better facing the other way." His moan was pitiful, and only made her lips twitch. "Of course, that would mean the coffee table and those two accent pieces would have to shift. And the palm tree—isn't it a beauty?—would have to go there."

The beauty weighed fifty pounds if it weighed an ounce. Cade abandoned pride and whined. "I still have stitches," he reminded her.

"Ah, what's a few stitches to a big, strong man like you?" She fluttered at him, patted his cheek and watched his ego war with his sore back. Giving in, she let loose a long, rolling laugh. "Gotcha. It's fine, darling, absolutely fine. You don't have to carry another cushion."

"You mean it?" His eyes went puppylike with hope. "It's done?"

"Not only is it done, but you're going to sit down, put up your feet, while I go get you an icy beer that

I stocked in my fridge just for tall, handsome private investigators."

"You're a goddess."

"So I've been told. Make yourself at home. I'll be right back."

When Grace came back bearing a tray, she saw that Cade had taken her invitation to heart. He sat back on the thick cobalt-blue cushions of her new U-shaped sofa arrangement, his feet propped on the mirror-bright surface of the ebony coffee table, his eyes shut.

"I really did wear you out, didn't I?"

He grunted, opened one eye. Then both popped open in appreciation when she set the loaded tray on the table. "Food," he said, and sprang for it.

She had to laugh as he dived into her offer of glossy green grapes, Brie and crackers, the heap of caviar on ice with toast points. "It's the least I can do for such an attractive moving man." Settling beside him, she picked up the glass of wine she'd poured for herself. "I owe you, Cade."

With his mouth half-full, he scanned the living room, nodded. "Damn straight."

"I don't just mean the manual labor. You gave me a safe haven when I needed one. And most of all, I owe you for Bailey."

"You don't owe me for Bailey. I love her."

"I know. So do I. I've never seen her happier. She

was just waiting for you." Leaning over, Grace kissed his cheek. "I always wanted a brother. Now, with you and Jack, I have two. Instant family. They fit, too, don't they?" she commented. "M.J. and Jack. As if they've always been a team."

"They keep each other on their toes. It's fun to watch."

"It is. And speaking of Jack, I thought he was going to give you a hand with our little redecorating project."

Cade scooped caviar onto a piece of toast. "He had a skip to trace."

"A what?"

"A bail jumper to bring in. He didn't think it was going to take him long." Cade swallowed, sighed. "He doesn't know what he's missing."

"I'll give him the chance to find out." She smiled. "I still have plans for a couple of the rooms upstairs."

It gave Cade his opening. "You know, Grace, I wonder if you're rushing this a little. It's going to take some time to put a house this size back in shape. Bailey and I would like you to stay at our place for a while."

Their place, Grace mused. Already it was their place. "It's more than livable here, Cade. M.J. and I talked about it," she continued. "She and Jack are going to her apartment. It's time we all got back to our routines."

But M.J. wasn't going to be alone, Cade thought, and thoughtfully sipped his beer. "There's still somebody pulling the strings out there. Somebody who wants the Three Stars."

"I don't have them," Grace reminded him. "I can't get them. There's no reason to bother with me at this point."

"I don't know how much reason has to do with it, Grace. I don't like you being here alone."

"Just like a brother." Delighted with him, she gave his arm a squeeze. "Listen, Cade, I've got a new alarm system, and I'm considering buying a big, mean, ugly dog." She started to mention the pistol she had in her nightstand, and the fact that she knew how to use it, but thought that would only worry him more. "I'll be fine."

"What does Buchanan think?"

"I haven't asked him. He's going to come by later— so I won't really be alone."

Satisfied with that, Cade handed her a grape. "You've got him worried."

Her lips curved as she popped the grape into her mouth. "Do I?"

"I don't know him well—I don't think anyone does. He's… I guess *self-contained* would be the word. Doesn't let a lot show on the surface. But when I walked in yesterday, after you'd gone upstairs, he was just standing there, looking up after you." Now Cade grinned. "There was plenty on the surface then. It was pretty illuminating. Seth Buchanan, human being."

Then he winced, tipped back his beer. "Sorry, I didn't mean to—"

"It's all right. I know exactly what you mean. He's got an almost terrifying self control, and that impenetrable aura of authority."

"It seems to me that you've managed to dent the armor. In my opinion, that's just what he needed. You're just what he needed."

"I hope he thinks so. It turns out he's just what I needed. I'm in love with him." With a half laugh, she shook her head and sipped her wine. "I can't believe I told you that. I rarely tell men my secrets."

"Brothers are different."

She smiled at him. "Yes, they are."

"I hope Seth appreciates just how lucky he is."

"I don't think Seth believes in luck."

She suspected Seth didn't believe in the Three Stars of Mithra, either. And she had discovered that she did. In a very short time, she'd simply opened her mind, stretched her imagination and accepted. They had magic, and they had power. She had been touched by both—as had Bailey and M.J. and the men who were linked to them.

Grace had no doubt that whoever wanted that magic, that power, would stop at nothing to gain them. It wouldn't matter when they were in the museum. He would still crave them, still plot to possess them.

But he could no longer reach the stones through her. That part of her connection, she thought with relief, was over. She was safe in her own home, and would learn to live there again. Starting now.

She dressed carefully in a long white dress of thin watered silk that left her shoulders bare and flirted with her ankles. Beneath the flowing silk she wore only skin, creamed and scented.

She left her hair loose, scooped back at the sides with silver combs, her mother's sapphire drops at her ears, gleaming like twin stars. On impulse, she'd clasped a thick silver bracelet high on her forearm—a touch of pagan.

When she looked into the mirror after dressing, she'd felt an odd jolt—as if she could see herself in the glass, with the faint ghost of someone else merged with her.

But she'd laughed it off, chalked it up to nerves and anticipation, and busied herself completing her preparations.

She filled the rooms she'd redone with candles and flowers, pleased with the welcome they offered. On the table by the window facing her side garden she arranged the china and crystal for her meticulously plotted dinner for two.

The champagne was iced, the music was on low and the lights were romantically dimmed. All she needed was the man.

* * *

Seth saw the candles in the windows when he pulled up in the drive. Fatigue layered over frustration and had him, in the dim light of the car, rubbing gritty eyes.

And there were candles in the windows.

He was forced to admit that for the first time in his adult life he didn't have a handle on himself, or on the world around him. He certainly didn't have a handle on the woman who had lit those candles, and who was waiting in that soft, flickering light.

He'd moved on DeVane on pure instinct—and part of that instinct, he knew, was territorial. Nothing could have been more out of character for him. Perhaps that was why he was feeling slightly…out of himself. Out of control. Grace had become a center, a focal point.

Or was it an obsession?

Hadn't he come here because he couldn't keep away? Just as he had dug into DeVane's background because the man roused some primal defense mechanism.

Maybe that was how it started, Seth admitted, but his cop's instincts were still honed. DeVane was dirty. And with a little more time, a little more digging, he would link the man with the deaths surrounding the diamonds.

Without the diplomatic block, Seth thought, he had enough already to bring the man in for questioning. DeVane liked to collect—and he collected the rare, the precious, and frequently those items that held some whiff of magic.

And Gregor DeVane had financed an expedition the year before to search for the legendary Stars. A rival archaeologist had found them first, and the Washington museum had acquired them.

DeVane had lost more than two million dollars on the hunt and the Stars had slipped through his fingers.

And the rival archaeologist had met with a tragic and fatal accident three months after the find, in the jungles of Costa Rica.

Seth didn't believe in coincidence. The man who had kept DeVane from possessing the diamonds was dead. And so, Seth had discovered, was the head of the expedition DeVane had put together.

No, he didn't believe in coincidence.

DeVane had been a resident of D.C. for nearly two years, on and off, without ever meeting Grace. Now, directly after Grace's connection with the Stars, the man was not only at the same social function, but happened to make a play for her?

Life simply wasn't that tidy.

A little more time, Seth promised himself, rubbing his temples to clear the headache. He'd find the solid connection—link DeVane to the Salvinis, to the bail bondsman, to the men who had died in a crashed van, to Carlo Monturri. He needed only one link, and then the rest of the chain would fall into place.

But at the moment, he needed to get out of the stuffy car, go inside and face what was happening to his personal life.

With a short laugh, Seth climbed out of the car. A personal life. Wasn't that part of the problem? He'd never had one, hadn't allowed himself one. Now, a matter of days after he'd met Grace, it was threatening to swallow him.

He needed time there, too, he told himself. Time to step back, gain some distance for a more objective look. He'd allowed things to move too fast, to get out of control. That would have to be fixed. A man who fell in love overnight couldn't trust himself. It was time to reassert some logic.

They were dynamically different—in backgrounds, in life-styles and in goals. Physical attraction was bound to fade, or certainly stabilize. He could already foresee her easing back once the initial excitement peaked. She'd grow restless, certainly annoyed with the demands on his work. He would be neither willing nor able to spin her through the social whirl that was such an intricate part of her life.

She was bound to look toward someone else who would. A beautiful woman, vital, sought-after, flattered at every turn, wouldn't be content to light a candle in the window for many nights.

He'd be doing them both a favor by slowing down, stepping back. As he lifted a hand to the gleaming brass knocker, he refused to hear the mocking voice inside his head that called him a liar—and a coward.

She answered the knock quickly, as if she'd only been waiting for it. She stood in the doorway, soft light filtering through the long flow of white silk. The power of her, pure and pagan, stopped his breath.

Though he kept his arms at his sides, she moved into him, and ripped at his heart with a welcoming kiss.

"It's good to see you." Grace skimmed her fingers along his cheekbones, under his shadowed eyes. "You've had a long one, Lieutenant. Come in and relax."

"I haven't got a lot of time. I've got work." He waited, saw the flicker of disappointment in her eyes. It helped justify what he was determined to do. But then she smiled, took his hand.

"Well, let's not waste what time you've got standing in the foyer. You haven't eaten, have you?"

Why didn't she ask him why he couldn't stay? he wondered, irrationally irritated. Why wasn't she complaining? "No."

"Good. Sit down and have a drink. Can you have a drink, or are you officially on duty?" She walked into the living area as she spoke, then drew the chilling champagne from its silver bucket. "I don't suppose one glass would matter, in any case. And I won't tell." She released the cork with an expert's twist and a muffled, celebratory pop. "I've just put the canapés out, so help yourself."

She gestured toward the silver tray on the coffee table before moving off with a quiet, slippery rustle of silk to pour two flutes.

"Tell me what you think. I worked poor Cade to death pushing things around in here, but I wanted to get at least the living space in order again quickly."

It looked as if it had been clipped from a glossy magazine on perfect living. Nothing was out of place, everything was gleaming and lovely. Bold colors mixed with whites and blacks, tasteful knickknacks, and artwork that appeared to have been selected with incredible care over a long period of time.

Yet she'd done it in days—or hours. That, Seth supposed, was the power of wealth and breeding.

Yet the room didn't look calculated or cold. It looked generous and welcoming. Soft surfaces, soft edges, with touches that were so Grace everywhere. Antique bottles in jewel tones, a china cat curled up for a nap, a lush, thriving fern in a copper pot.

And flowers, candlelight.

He looked up, noted the unbroken gleam of wood circling the balcony. "I see you've had it repaired."

Something's wrong, was all she could think as she stepped forward and handed him his glass. "Yes, I wanted that done as soon as possible. That, and the new security system. I think you'll approve."

"I'll take a look at it, if you like."

"I'd like it better if you'd relax while you can. Why don't I bring dinner in?"

"You cooked?"

Now she laughed. "I wouldn't do that to you, but I'm an expert at ordering in—and at presentation. Try to unwind. I'll be right back."

As she glided out, he looked down at the tray. A silver bowl of glossy black caviar, little fancy bites of elegant finger foods. He turned his back on them and, carrying his glass, walked over to study her portrait.

When she came back, wheeling an antique cart, he continued to look at her painted face. "He was in love with you, wasn't he? The artist?"

Grace drew a careful breath at that cool tone. "Yes, he was. He knew I didn't love him. I often wished I could have. Charles is one of the kindest, gentlest men I know."

"Did you sleep with him?"

A chill snaked up her spine, but she kept her hands steady as she set plates on the candle- and flower-decked table. "No. It wouldn't have been fair, and I care about him too much."

"You'd rather sleep with men you don't care about."

She hadn't seen it coming, Grace realized. How foolish of her not to have seen this coming. "No, but I won't sleep with men who I could hurt like that. I would have hurt Charles by being his lover, so I stayed his friend."

"And the wives?" He did turn now, eyes narrowed as he studied the woman instead of the portrait. "Like the woman who was married to that earl you were mixed up with? Didn't you worry about hurting her?"

Grace picked up her wine again, quite deliberately cocked her head. She had never slept with the earl he'd mentioned, or with any other married man. But she had never bothered to argue with public perception. Nor would she bother to deny it now.

"Why would I? I wasn't married to her."

"And the guy who tried to kill himself after you broke your engagement?"

She touched the glass to her lips, swallowed frothy wine that burned like shards of glass in her throat. "Overly dramatic of him, wasn't it? I don't think you're in the mood for Caesar salad and steak Diane, are you, Lieutenant? Rich food doesn't set well during interrogations."

"No one's interrogating you, Grace."

"Oh, yes, you are. But you neglected to read me my rights."

Her frigid anger helped justify his own. It wasn't the men—he knew it wasn't the men he'd very deliberately tossed in her face that scraped at him. It was the fact that they didn't matter to him, that somehow nothing seemed to matter but her.

"It's odd you're so sensitive about answering questions about men, Grace. You hadn't troubled to hide your...track record."

"I expected better from you." She said it softly, so he barely heard, then shook her head, smiled coolly. "Foolish of me. No, I've never troubled to hide anything—unless it mattered. The men didn't matter, for the most part. Do you want me to tell you that you're different? Would you believe me if I did?"

He was afraid he would. Terrified he would. "It isn't necessary. We've moved too fast, Grace. I'm not comfortable with it."

"I see." She thought she did now, perfectly. "You'd like to slow things down." She set her glass aside, knowing her hand would start to shake. "It appears you've taken a couple of those giant steps while I've had my back turned. I really should have played that game as a child, so I'd be more alert for sudden moves."

"This isn't a game."

"No, I suppose it isn't." She had her pride, but she

also had her heart. And she had to know. "How could you have made love with me like that this morning, Seth, and do this tonight? How could you have touched me the way you have—the way no one ever has—and hurt me like this?"

It was because of what had swamped him that morning, he realized. The helplessness of his need. "I'm not trying to hurt you."

"No, that only makes it worse. You're doing both of us a favor, aren't you? Isn't that how you've worked it out? Break things off before they get too messy? Too late." Her voice broke, but she managed to shore it up again. "It's already messy."

"Damn it." He took a step toward her, then stopped dead when her head whipped up, and those hot blue eyes scorched him.

"Don't even think about touching me now, when those thoughts are still in your head. You go your tidy way, Lieutenant, and I'll go mine. I don't believe in slowing down. You either go forward, or you stop."

Furious with herself, she lifted a hand and flicked a tear off her cheek. "Apparently, we've stopped."

Chapter 11

He stood there wondering what in the hell he was doing. Here was the woman he loved, who—by some wild twist of fate—might actually love him. Here was a chance for that life he'd never allowed himself, the family, the home, the woman. He was pushing them all away, with both hands, and couldn't seem to stop.

"Grace... I want to give us both time to consider what we're doing, where this is going."

"No, you don't." She tossed back her hair with one angry jerk of her head. "Do you think because I've only known you a matter of days that I don't understand how your head works? I've been more intimate with you than I've been with anyone in my life. I *know* you." She managed a deep, ragged breath. "What you want is to get that wheel back under your hands, that control button back under your thumb. This whole thing has run away from you, and you just can't let that happen."

"That may be true." Was true, he realized. Was absolutely, mortifyingly true. "But it doesn't change the point. I'm in the middle of an investigation, and I'm not as objective as I need to be, because I'm involved with you. After it's done—"

"After it's done, what?" she demanded. "We pick up where you left off? I don't think so, Lieutenant. What happens when you're in the middle of the next investigation? And the next? Do I strike you as someone who's going to wait around until you have the time, and the room, to continue an on-again, off-again relationship with me?"

"No." His spine stiffened. "I'm a cop, and my work takes priority."

"I don't believe I've ever asked you to change that. In fact, I found your dedication to your work admirable, attractive. Even heroic." Her smile was thin and brief. "But that's irrelevant, and so is this conversation." She turned away, picked up her wine again. "You know the way out."

No, she'd never asked him to change anything. Never questioned his work. What the hell had he done? "This needs to be discussed."

"That's your style, not mine. Do you actually think you can stand here, in my home…" Her voice began to hitch and jerk. "In my home, and break my heart, dump me and expect a civilized conversation? I want you *out*." She slammed her glass down, snapping the fragile stem of the glass, splattering wine. "Right now."

Where had the panic come from? he wondered. His beeper went off and was ignored. "We're not leaving it this way."

"Exactly this way," she corrected. "Do you think I'm stupid? Do you think I don't see that you walked in here tonight looking to pick a fight so that it would end exactly this way? Do you think I don't know now that no matter how much I gave you, you'd hold back from me, question, analyze, dissect everything? Well, analyze this. I was willing to give more, whatever you wanted to take. Now you can spend the rest of your life wondering just what you lost here tonight."

As his beeper sounded again, she swept by him, wrenched open the front door. "You'll have to answer that call of duty elsewhere, Lieutenant."

He stepped to her, but, though his arms ached, he resisted the need to reach out. "When I'm done with this, I'm coming back."

"You won't be welcome."

He could feel himself step up to a line he'd never crossed. "That isn't going to matter. I'm coming back."

She said nothing at all, simply shut the door in his face and turned the lock with a hard, audible click.

She leaned back against the door, her breath shallow now, and hot, as pain swept through her. It was worse now that the door was closed, now that she had shut him out. And the candles still flickered, the flowers still bloomed.

She saw that every step she'd taken that day, and the day before, all they way back to the moment she'd walked into her own home and seen him coming down the stairs toward her, had been leading to this moment of blind grief and loss.

She'd been powerless to stop it, she thought, to change what she was, what had come before or what would come after. It was only fools who believed they controlled their own destiny as she'd once believed she controlled hers.

And she'd been a fool to indulge in those pathetic fantasies, dreams where they had belonged together, where they'd made a life together, a home and children together. Where she'd believed she was only waiting for him to finally make all those longings that had always, always, been one handspan out of her reach, come true.

The mythical power of the stones, she thought with a half laugh. Love, knowledge and generosity. Their magic had been cruel to her, giving her that tantalizing glimpse of her every desire, then wrenching it away again and leaving her alone.

The knock on the door had her closing her eyes. How dare he come back, she thought. How dare he, after he'd smashed all her dreams, her hopes, her needs. And how dare she still love him in spite of it.

Well, he wouldn't see her cry, she promised herself, and straightened to scrub her hands over her damp cheeks. He wouldn't see her crawl. He wouldn't see her at all, because she wouldn't let him in.

Resolutely she headed for the phone. He wouldn't be pleased when she called 911 and reported an intruder, she mused. But it would make her point. She picked up the receiver just as the sound of shattering glass had her whirling toward her terrace doors.

She had time to see the man burst through them, time to hear her alarm scream in warning. She even had time to struggle as thick arms grabbed her. Then the cloth was over her face, smelling sickeningly of chloroform.

And she had time only to think of Seth before her world spun and went black.

Seth was barely three miles away when the next call came through. He jerked up his phone, snarled into it. "Buchanan."

"Lieutenant, Detective Marshall again. I just heard an automatic come through on dispatch. Suspected break-in, 2918 East Lark Lane, Potomac."

"What?" For one stunning moment, his mind went blank. "Grace?"

"I recognized the address from the homicide. Her alarm system's been triggered, she didn't answer the check-in call."

"I'm five minutes from there." He was already swinging around in a fast, tire-squealing turn. "Get the two closest black-and-whites on the scene. Now."

"I'm already on it. Lieutenant—"

But Seth had already tossed the phone aside.

It was a new system, Seth told himself, fighting for calm and logic. New systems often had glitches.

She was upset, not answering her phone, ignoring the confusion. It would be just like her. She was even now defiantly pouring herself another glass of champagne, cursing him.

Maybe she'd even set off the alarm herself, just so he'd come streaking back with his stomach encased in ice and his heart paralyzed. It would be just like her.

And that was one more lie, he thought as he careened around a corner. It was nothing like her at all.

The candles were still burning in her windows. He tried to be relieved by that as he stood on the brakes in her driveway and bolted out of his car. Dinner would still be warm, the music would still be playing, and Grace would be there, standing under her portrait, furious with him.

He beat on the door foolishly, wildly, before he snapped himself back. She wouldn't answer. She was too angry to answer. When the first patrol car pulled up, he turned, flashed his badge.

"Check the east side," he ordered. "I'll take the west."

He turned on his heel, started around the side. He caught the glimmer of the blue water in her pool in the moonlight, and the thought slid in and out of his mind that they'd never used it together, never slipped into that cool water naked.

Then he saw the broken glass. His heart simply stopped. His weapon was in his hand and he was through the shattered door, with no thought to procedure. Someone was shouting her name, racing from room to room in blind panic. It couldn't be him, yet he found himself on the stairs, short of breath, ice cold, dizzy with fear and watching a uniformed cop bend to pick up a scrap of cloth.

"Smells like chloroform, Lieutenant." The officer hesitated, took a step toward the man clinging to the banister. "Lieutenant?"

He couldn't speak. His voice was gone, and every sweaty hour of training with it. Seth's dulled gaze shifted, focused on the face, the portrait. Slowly, and with great effort, he widened his vision again, pulled on the mask of control.

"Search the house. Every inch of it." His eyes locked

on the second uniform. "Call in for backup. Now. Then make a sweep of the grounds. Move."

Grace came to slowly, with a roll of nausea and a blinding headache. A nightmare, still black at the edges, circled dully, like a vulture patiently waiting to drop. She squeezed her eyes tighter, rolled her head on the pillow, then cautiously opened them.

Where? The thought was dull, foolish. Not my room, she realized, and struggled to fight off the clinging mists that clouded her brain.

It was satin beneath her cheek. She knew the cool, slippery feel of satin against the skin. White satin, like a bride's dress. Baffled, she skimmed her hand over the thick, luxurious spread of the huge canopied bed.

She could smell jasmine, and roses, and vanilla. All white scents, cool white scents. The walls of the room were ivory and had a sheen like silk. For a moment, she thought she was in a coffin, a huge, elaborate coffin, and her heart beat thick and fast.

She made herself sit up, almost afraid that her head would hit the lid and she would find herself screaming and clawing for freedom as she smothered. But there was nothing, only that fragrant air, and she took a long, unsteady breath of it.

She remembered now—the crash of glass, the big man in black with thick arms. She wanted to panic and forced herself to take another of those jerky breaths. Carefully, hampered by her spinning head, she slid her legs over the edge of the bed until her feet sank into thick, virginal white carpet. She swayed, nearly retched, then forced her feet over that sea of white to the door.

She went slippery with panic when the knob resisted her. Her breath came in ragged gulps as she fought and tugged on the knob of faceted crystal. Then she turned her back, leaned against it and made herself survey what she understood now was her prison.

White on white on white, blinding to the eye. A dainty Queen Anne chair brocaded in white, filmy lace curtains hung like ghosts, heaps of white pillows on a curved white chaise. There were edges of gold that only enhanced the avalanche of white, elegant furniture in pale wood smothered in that snowfall.

She went to the windows first, shuddered when she found them barred, the slices of night beyond them silvered by the moon. She saw nothing familiar—a long roll of lawn, meticulously planted flowers and shrubs, tall, shielding trees.

Wheeling, she saw another door, bolted for it, nearly wept when the knob turned easily. But beyond was a lustrous bath, white-tiled, the frosted-glass windows barred, the angled skylight a soaring ten feet above the floor.

And on the long gleaming counter were jars, bottles, creams, powders. All her own preferences, her scents, her lotions. Her stomach knotted greasily.

Ransom, she told herself. It was a kidnapping, someone who believed her family could be forced to pay for her safe return.

But she knew that was a lie.

The Stars. She leaned weakly against the jamb, pressed her lips together to keep the whimper silent. She'd been taken because of the Three Stars. They would be her ransom.

Her knees trembled as she turned away, ordered herself to calm down, to think clearly. There had to be a way out. There always was.

Her alarm had gone off, she remembered. Seth couldn't have been far away. Would he have gotten the report, come back? It didn't matter. He would have gotten it soon enough. Whatever had happened between them, he would do everything in his power to find her. From duty, if nothing else.

In the meantime, she was on her own. But that didn't mean she was defenseless.

She took two stumbling steps back when the lock on her door clicked, then forced herself to stop, straighten. The door opened, and two men stepped inside. One she recognized quickly enough as her abductor. The other was smaller, wiry, dressed in formal black, with a face as giving as rock.

"Ms. Fontaine," he said in a voice both British and cultured. "If you'd come with me, please."

A butler, she realized, and had to swallow a bubble of hysteria. She knew the type too well, and she assumed an amused and annoyed expression. "Why?"

"He's ready to see you now."

When she made no move to obey, the bigger man stepped in, towering over her, then jerked a thumb toward the doorway.

"Charming," she said dryly. She took a step forward, calculating how quickly she would have to move. The butler inclined his head impassively.

"You're on the third floor," he told her. "Even if you could somehow reach the main level on your own, there are guards. They are under order not to harm you, unless it's unavoidable. If you'll pardon me, I would advise against risking it."

She would risk it, she thought, and a great deal more. But not until she had at least an even chance of success. Without so much as a flick of a glance at the man beside her, she followed the butler out of the room and down a gently lit corridor.

The house was old, she calculated, but beautifully restored. At least three stories, so it was large. A glimpse at her watch told her it had been less than two hours since she was drugged. Time enough to drive some distance, she imagined.

But the view through the bars hadn't been country-side. She'd seen lights—city lights, houses through the trees. A neighborhood, she decided. Exclusive, wealthy, but a neighborhood.

Where there were houses, there were people. And where there were people, there was help.

She was led down a wide, curving staircase of gleaming oak. And saw the guard at the landing, his gun holstered but visible.

Down another hallway. Antiques, paintings, artwork. Her eye was expert enough to recognize the Monet on the wall, the porcelain vase from the Han dynasty on a pedestal, the Nok terra-cotta head from Nigeria.

Her host, she thought, had excellent and eclectic taste. The treasures she saw, small and large, spanned continents and centuries.

A collector, she realized with a chill. Now he had her, and was hoping to trade her for the Three Stars of Mithra.

With what Grace considered absurd formality, under the circumstances, the butler approached tall double doors, opened them, and with seamless expertise bowed slightly from the waist.

"Miss Grace Fontaine."

Seeing no immediate alternative, she stepped

through the open doors into an enormous dining room with a frescoed ceiling and a dazzling trio of chandeliers. She scanned the long mahogany table, the Georgian candelabra gaily lit and spaced at precise intervals down its length, and focused on the man who rose and smiled charmingly.

Her worlds overlapped—reality and fear. "Gregor."

"Grace." Elegant in his tux, diamonds winking, he crossed to her, took her numb hand in his. "How delightful to see you." He tucked her arm through his, patted it affectionately. "I don't believe you've dined."

He knew where she was. Seth had no doubt of it, but his first fiery urge to rush to the elegant estate in D.C. and tear it apart single-handedly had to be suppressed.

He could get her killed.

He was certain Ambassador Gregor DeVane had killed before.

The call that interrupted his scene with Grace had been confirmation of yet another woman who had once been linked to the ambassador, a beautiful German scientist who had been found murdered in her home in Berlin, the apparent victim of a bungled burglary.

The dead woman had been an anthropologist who had a keen interest in Mithraism. For six months during the previous year, she had been romantically linked with Gregor DeVane. Then she was dead, and none of her research notes on the Three Stars of Mithra had been recovered.

He knew DeVane was responsible, just as he knew DeVane had Grace. But he couldn't prove it, and he didn't have probable cause to sway any judge to issue a search warrant into the home of a foreign ambassador.

Once more he stood in Grace's living room. Once more he stared up at her portrait and imagined her dead. But this time, he wasn't thinking like a cop.

He turned as Mick Marshall stepped beside him. "We won't find anything here to link him. In twelve hours, the diamonds will be turned over to the museum. He's going to use her to see that doesn't happen. I'm going to stop him."

Mick looked up at the portrait. "What do you need?"

"No. No cops."

"Lieutenant… Seth, if you're right, and he's got her, you're not going to get her out alone. You need to put together a team. You need a hostage negotiator."

"There's no time. We both know that." His eyes weren't flat and cool now, weren't cop's eyes. They were full of storms and passions. "He'll kill her."

His heart was coated with a sheet of ice, but it beat with fiery heat inside the casing. "She's smart. She'll play whatever game she needs to in order to stay alive, but if she makes the wrong move he'll kill her. I don't need a psychiatric profile to see into his head. He's a sociopath with a god complex and an obsession. He wants those diamonds and what he believes they represent. Right now he wants Grace, but if she doesn't serve his purpose, she'll end up like the others. That's not going to happen, Mick."

He reached into his pocket, took out his badge and held it out. This time he wouldn't go by the book, couldn't afford to play by the rules. "You take this for me, hang on to it. I may want it back."

"You're going to need help," Mick insisted. "You're going to need men."

"No cops," Seth repeated, and pushed his badge into Mick's reluctant hand. "Not this time."

"You can't go in solo. It's suicide, professional and literal."

Seth cast one last glance at the portrait. "I won't be alone."

She wouldn't tremble, Grace promised herself. She wouldn't show him how frightened she was. Instead, she brushed her hair from her shoulder with a careless hand.

"Do you always have your dinner companions abducted from their homes and drugged, Ambassador?"

"You must forgive the clumsiness." Considerately he drew out a chair for her. "It was necessary to be quick. I trust you're suffering no ill effects."

"Other than great annoyance, no." She sat, skimmed her gaze over the dish of marinated mushrooms a silent servant placed before her. They reminded her, painfully, of the noise-filled cookout at Cade's. "And a loss of appetite."

"Oh, you must at least sample the food." He sat at the head of the table, picked up his fork. It was gold and heavy and had once slipped between the lips of an emperor. "I've gone to considerable trouble to have your favorites prepared." His smile remained genial, but his eyes went cold. "Eat, Grace. I detest waste."

"Since you've gone to such lengths." She forced down a bite, ordered her hand not to shake, her stomach not to revolt.

"I hope your room is comfortable. I had to have it prepared for you rather quickly. You'll find appropriate clothing in the armoire and bureau. You've only to ask if there's something else you wish."

"I prefer windows without bars, and doors without locks."

"Temporary precautions, I promise you. Once you're at home here…" His hand covered hers, the grip tightening cruelly when she attempted to pull away. "…and I do very much want you to be at home here, such measures won't be necessary."

She didn't wince as the bones in her hand ground

together. When she stopped the resistance, his fingers relaxed, stroked once, then slid away.

"And just how long do you intend to keep me here?"

He smiled, picked up her wineglass, held it out to her. "Eternity. You and I, Grace, are destined to share eternity."

Under the table, her aching hand shook and went clammy. "That's quite some time." She started to set her wine down, untouched, then caught the hard glint in his eye and sipped. "I'm flattered, but confused."

"It's pointless to pretend you don't understand. You held the Star in your hand. You survived death, and you came to me. I've seen your face in my dreams."

"Yes." She could feel her blood drain slowly, as if leeched out of her veins. Looking into his eyes she remembered the nightmares—the shadow in the woods. Watching. "I've seen you in mine."

"You'll bring me the Stars, Grace, and the power. I understand why I failed now. Every step was simply another on the path that brought us here. Together we'll possess the Stars. And I will possess you. Don't worry," he said when she flinched. "You'll come to me a willing bride. But my patience has limits. Beauty is my weakness," he continued, and skimmed a fingertip down her bare arm, toyed idly with the thick silver bracelet she wore. "And perfection my greatest delight. You, my dear, have both. Understand, you'll have no choice should my patience run out. My household staff is…well trained."

Fear was a bright, icy flash, but her voice was steady with disgust. "And would turn a deaf ear and blind eye to rape?"

"I don't enjoy that word during dinner." He gave a sulky little shrug and signaled for the next course. "A woman of your appetites will grow hungry soon enough. And one of your intelligence will undoubtedly see the wisdom of an amiable partnership."

"It's not sex you want, Gregor." She couldn't bear to look down at the tender pink salmon on her plate. "It's subjugation. I'm so poor at subjugation."

"You misunderstand me." He forked up fish and ate with enjoyment. "I intend to make you a goddess, and subject to no one. And I will have everything. No mortal man will come between us." He smiled again. "Certainly not Lieutenant Buchanan. The man is becoming a nuisance. He's probing into my affairs, where he has no business probing. I've seen him…"

DeVane's voice trailed off to a whisper, and there was a hint of fear in it. "In the night. In my dreams. He comes back. He always comes back. No matter how often I kill him." Then his eyes cleared, and he sipped wine the color of melted gold. "Now he's stirring up old business and looking for new."

She could feel the alarming beat of her pulse in her

throat, at her wrists, in her temples. "He'll be looking for me, very soon now."

"Possibly. I'll deal with him, when and if the time comes. That could have been tonight, had he not left you so abruptly. Oh, I have considered just what will be done about the lieutenant. But I prefer to wait until I have the Stars. It's possible..." Thoughtfully DeVane picked up his napkin, dabbed at his lips. "I may spare him once I have what belongs to me. If you wish it. I can be magnanimous...under the right circumstances."

Her heart was in her throat now, filling it, blocking it. "If I do what you want, you'll leave him alone?"

"It's possible. We'll discuss it. But I'm afraid I developed an immediate dislike for the man. And I am still annoyed with you, dear Grace, for rejecting my own invitation for such an ordinary man."

She didn't hesitate, couldn't afford to, while her mind whirled with fear for Seth. She made her lips curve silkily. "Gregor, surely you forgive me for that. I was so...crushed when you didn't press your case. A woman, after all, enjoys a more determined pursuit."

"I don't pursue. I take."

"Obviously." She pouted. "It was horrid of you to have manhandled me that way, and frightened me half to death. I may not forgive you for it."

"Be careful how deep you play the game." His voice

was low with warning and, she thought, with interest. "I'm not green."

"No." She skimmed a hand over his cheek before she rose. "But maturity has so many advantages."

Her legs were watery, but she roamed the cavernous room, her gaze traveling quickly toward windows, exits. Escape. "You have such a beautiful home. So many treasures." She angled her head, hoped the challenge she issued was worth the risk. "I do love... things. But I warn you, Gregor, I won't be any man's pretty toy."

She walked to him slowly, skimming a fingertip down her throat, between her breasts, while the silk she wore whispered around her. "And when I'm backed into a corner... I scratch."

Seductively she laid a hand on the table, leaned toward him. "You want me?" she breathed it, purred it, watching his eyes darken, sliding her fingers toward the knife beside his plate. "To touch me? To have me?" Her fingers closed over the handle, gripped hard.

"Not in a hundred lifetimes," she said as she struck.

She was fast, and she was desperate. But he'd shifted to draw her to him, and the knife struck his shoulder instead of his heart. As he cried out in shock and rage, she whirled. Grabbing one of the heavy chairs, she smashed the long window and sent glass raining out.

But when she leaped forward, strong arms grabbed her from behind.

She fought viciously, her breath panting out. The fragile silk she wore ripped. Then she froze when the knife she had used was pressed against her throat. She didn't bother to struggle against the arms that held her as DeVane leaned his face close to hers. His eyes were mad with fury.

"I could kill you for that. But it would be too little and too quick. I would have made you my equal. I would have shared that with you. Now I'll just take what I choose from you. Until I tire of you."

"You'll never get the Stars," she said steadily. "And you'll never get Seth."

"I'll have exactly what I choose. And you'll help me."

She started to shake her head, flinched as the blade nicked. "I'll do nothing to help you."

"But you will. If you don't do exactly as I tell you, I will pick up the phone. With one single word from me, Bailey James and M. J. O'Leary will die tonight. It will only take a word."

He saw the wild fear come into her eyes, the helpless terror that hadn't been there for her own life. "I have men waiting for that word. If I give it, there will be a terrible and tragic explosion in the night at Cade Parris's home. Another at a small neighborhood pub, just before closing. And as one last twist, a third explosion will destroy the home, and the single occupant, of a certain Lieutenant Buchanan's residence. Their fate is in your hands, Grace. And the choice is yours."

She wanted to call his bluff, but, staring into his eyes, she understood that he wouldn't hesitate to do as he threatened. No, he longed to do it. Their lives meant nothing to him. And everything to her.

"What do you want me to do?"

Bailey was fighting against panic when the phone rang. She stared at it as if it were a snake that had rattled into life. With a silent prayer, she lifted the receiver. "Hello?"

"Bailey."

"Grace." Her fingers went white-knuckled as she whirled. Seth shook his head, held up a hand in caution. "Are you all right?"

"For the moment. Listen very carefully, Bailey, my life depends on it. Do you understand?"

"No. Yes." Stall, she knew she'd been ordered to stall. "Grace, I'm so frightened for you. What happened? Where are you?"

"I can't go into that now. You have to be calm, Bailey. You have to be strong. You were always the calm one. Like when we took that art history exam in college and I was so intimidated by Professor Greenbalm, and you were so cool. You have to be cool now, Bailey, and you have to follow my instructions."

"I will. I'll try." She looked helplessly at Seth as he signaled her to stretch it out. "Just tell me if you're hurt."

"Not yet. But he will hurt me. He'll kill me, Bailey, if you don't do what he wants. Get him what he wants. I know I'm asking a great deal. He wants the stones. You have to go get them. You can't take Cade. You can't call…the police."

String it out, Bailey reminded herself. Keep Grace talking. "You don't want me to call Seth?"

"No. He isn't important. He's just another cop. You know he doesn't matter. You're to wait until 1:30 exactly, then you're to leave the house. Go to Salvini, Bailey. You've got to go to Salvini. Leave M.J. out of it, just like we used to. Understand?"

Bailey nodded, kept her eyes on Seth's. "Yes, I understand."

"Once you get to Salvini, put the stones in a briefcase. Wait there. You'll get a call with the next set of instructions. You'll be all right. You know how you used to like to sneak out of the dorm at night and go out driving alone after curfew? Just think of it that way. Exactly that way, Bailey, and you'll be fine. If you don't, he'll take everything away from me. Do you understand?"

"Yes. Grace—"

"I love you," she managed before the phone went dead.

"Nothing," Cade said tightly as he stared down at the tracing equipment. "He's got it jammed. The signal's all over the board. It wouldn't home in."

"She wants me to go to Salvini," Bailey said quietly.

"You're not going anywhere," Cade said, interrupting her, but Bailey laid a hand on his arm, looked toward M.J.

"No, she meant that part. You understood?"

"Yeah." M.J. pressed her fingers to her eyes, tried to think past the terror. "She was pumping in as much as she could. Bailey and Grace never left me out of anything, so she wanted me along. She wants us out of here, but she was stringing him about the stones. Bailey never jumped curfew."

"She was giving you signals," Jack said. "Trying to punch in what she could manage."

"She knew we'd understand. He must have told her something would happen to us if she didn't cooperate." Bailey reached out for M.J.'s hand. "She wanted us to contact Seth. That's why she said you didn't matter— because we know you do."

Seth dragged a hand through his hair—a rare wasted motion. He had no choice but to trust their instincts. No choice but to trust Grace's sense of survival. "All right. She wants me to know what's happening, and wants you out of the house."

"Yes. She wants us out of the house, thinks we'll be safer at Salvini."

"You'll be safer at the precinct," Seth told her. "And that's where both of you are going."

"No." Bailey's voice remained calm. "She wants us at Salvini. She made a point of it."

Seth studied her, and gauged his options. He could have them taken into protective custody. That was the logical step. Or he could let the game play out. That was a risk. But it was the risk that fit.

"Salvini, then. But Detective Marshall will arrange for guards. You'll stay put until you hear differently."

M.J. bristled. "You expect us to just sit around and wait while Grace is in trouble?"

"That's exactly what you're going to do," Seth said coolly. "She's risking her life to see that you're safe. I'm not going to disappoint her."

"He's right, M.J." Jack lifted a brow as she snarled at him. "Go ahead and fume. But you're outnumbered here. You and Bailey follow instructions."

Seth noted with some surprise that M.J. closed her mouth, gave one brisk nod in assent. "What was the business about the art history exam, Bailey?"

Bailey sucked in air. "Professor Greenbalm's first name was Gregory."

"Gregory." *Gregor.* "Close enough." Seth looked at the two men he needed. "We don't have a lot of time."

Chapter 12

Grace doubted very much that she would live through the night. There were so many things she hadn't done. She had never shown Bailey and M.J. Paris, as they had always planned. She would never see the willow she'd planted on her country hillside grow tall and bend gracefully over her tiny pond. She had never had a child.

The unfairness clawed at her, along with the fear. She was only twenty-six years old, and she was going to die.

She'd seen her sentence in DeVane's eyes. And she knew he intended to kill those she loved, as well. He wouldn't be satisfied with anything less than erasing all the lives that had touched what his obsessed mind considered his.

All she could hang on to now was the hope that Bailey had understood her.

"I'm going to show you what you could have had." His arm bandaged, a fresh tuxedo covering the damage, DeVane led her through a concealed panel, and down a well-lit set of stone stairs that were polished like ebony. He'd taken a painkiller. His eyes were glassy with it, and vicious.

They were the eyes that had stared out of the woods in her nightmares. And as he walked down the curve of those glossy black stairs, she felt the tug of some deep memory.

By torchlight then, she thought hazily. Down and down, with the torches flickering and the Stars glittering in their home of gold, on a white stone. And death waiting.

The harsh breathing of the man beside her. DeVane's? Someone else's? It was a hot, secret sound that chilled the skin. A room, she thought, struggling to grip the slippery chain of memories. A secret room of white and gold. And she had been locked in it for eternity.

She stopped at the last curve, not so much in fear as in shock. Not here, she thought frantically, but somewhere else. Not her, but part of her. Not him, but someone like him.

DeVane's fingers dug into her arm, but she barely

felt the pain. Seth—the man with Seth's eyes, dressed as a warrior, coated with dust and the dents of battle. He'd come for her, and for the Stars.

And died for it.

"No." The stairway spun, and she gripped the cool wall for balance. "Not again. Not this time."

"There's little choice." DeVane jerked her forward, pulled her down the remaining steps. He stopped at a thick door, gestured impatiently for his guard to step back. Holding Grace's arm in a bruising grip, he drew out a heavy key, fit it in an old lock that for reasons Grace couldn't fathom made her think of Alice's rabbit hole.

"I want you to see what could have been yours. What I would have shared with you."

At his rough shove, she stumbled inside and stood blinking in shock.

No, not the rabbit hole, she realized, her dazzled eyes wide and stunned. Ali Baba's cave. Gold gleamed in mountains, jewels winked in rivers. Paintings she recognized as works of the masters crowded together on the walls. Statues and sculpture, some as small as the Fabergé eggs perched on gold stands, others soaring to the ceiling, were jammed inside.

Furs and sweeps of silk, ropes of pearls, carvings and crowns, were jammed into every available space. Mozart played brilliantly on hidden speakers.

It was, she realized, not a fairy-tale cave at all. It was merely a spoiled boy's elaborate and greedy clubhouse. Here he could hide his possessions from the world, keep them all to himself and chortle over them, she imagined.

And how many of these toys had he stolen? she wondered. How many had he killed for?

She wouldn't die here, she promised herself. And neither would Seth. If this was indeed history overlapping, she wouldn't allow it to repeat itself. She would fight with whatever weapons she had.

"You have quite a collection, Gregor, but your presentation could use some work." The first weapon was mild disdain, laced with amusement. "Even the precious loses impact when crammed together in such a disorganized manner."

"It's mine. All of it. A lifetime's work. Here." Like that spoiled boy, he snatched up a goblet of gold, thrust it out to her for admiration. "Queen Guinevere sipped from this before she cuckolded Arthur. He should have cut out her heart for that."

Grace turned the cup in her hand and felt nothing. It was empty not only of wine, she mused, but of magic.

"And here." He grabbed a pair of ornate diamond earrings, thrust them into Grace's face. "Another queen—Marie Antoinette—wore these while her country plotted her death. You might have worn them."

"While you plotted mine." With deliberate scorn, she dismissed the offering and turned away. "No, thank you."

"I have an arrow the goddess Diana hunted with. The girdle worn by Juno."

Her heart thrummed like a harp, but she only chuckled. "Do you really believe that?"

"They're mine." Furious with her reaction, he pushed his way through his collection, laid a hand over the cold marble slab he'd had built. "I'll have the Stars soon. They will be the apex of my collection. I'll set them here, with my own hands. And I'll have everything."

"They won't help you. They won't change you." She didn't know where the words came from, or the knowledge behind them, but she saw his eyes flicker in surprise. "Your fate's already sealed. They'll never be yours. It's not meant, not this time. They're for the light, and for the good. You'll never see them here in the dark."

His stomach jittered. There was power in her words, in her eyes, when she should have been cowed and frightened. It unnerved him. "By sunrise I'll have them here. I'll show them to you." His breath was short and shallow as he approached her. "And I'll have you. I'll keep you as long as I wish. Do with you what I wish."

The hand against her cheek was cold, made her think wildly of a snake, but she didn't cringe away. "You'll never have the Stars, and you'll never have me. Even if you hold us, you'll never have us. That was true before, but it's only more true now. And that will eat away at you, day after day, until there's nothing left of you but madness."

He struck her, hard enough to knock her back against the wall, to have pain spinning in her head. "Your friends will die tonight." He smiled at her, as if he were discussing a small mutual interest. "You've already sent them to oblivion. I'm going to let you live a long time knowing that."

He took her by the arm and, pulling open the door, dragged her from the room.

"He'll have surveillance cameras," Seth said as they prepared to scale the wall at the rear of DeVane's D.C. estate. "He's bound to have guards patrolling the grounds."

"So we'll be careful." Jack checked the point of his knife, stuck it in his boot, then examined the pistol he'd tucked in his belt. "And we'll be quiet."

"We stick together until we reach the house." Cade went over the plan in his head. "I find security, disarm it."

"Failing that, set the whole damn business off. We

could get lucky in the confusion. It'll bring the cops. If things don't go well, you could be dealing with a lot more than a bust for a B-and-E."

Jack issued a pithy one-word opinion on that. "Let's go get her out." He shot Seth one quick grin as he boosted himself up. "Man, I hope he doesn't have dogs. I really hate when they have dogs."

They landed on the soft grass on the other side. It was possible their presence was detected from that moment. It was a risk they were willing to take. Like shadows, they moved through the starstruck night, slipping through the heavy dark amid the sheltering trees.

Before, on his quest for the Stars and the woman, he'd come alone, and perhaps that arrogance had been his defeat. Baffled by the sudden thought, the quick spurt of what some might have called vision, Seth pushed the feeling aside.

He could see the house through the trees, the glimmer of lights in windows. Which room was she in? How badly was she frightened? Was she hurt? Had he touched her?

Baring his teeth, he bit off the thoughts. He had to focus only on getting inside, finding her. For the first time in years, he felt the weight of his weapon at his side. Knew he intended to use it.

He gave no thought to rules, to his career, to the life he'd built step by deliberate step.

He saw the guard pass by, only a yard beyond the verge of the grove. When Jack tapped his shoulder and signaled, Seth met his eyes, nodded.

Seconds later, Jack sprang at the man from behind, and with a quick twist, rammed his head into the trunk of an oak and then dragged the unconscious body into the shadows.

"One down," he breathed and tucked his newly acquired weapon away.

"They'll have regular check-in," Cade murmured. "We can't know how soon they'll miss his contact."

"Then let's move." Seth signaled Jack to the north, Cade to the south. Staying low, they rushed those gleaming lights.

The guard who escorted Grace back to her room was silent. At least two hundred and fifty pounds of muscle, she calculated. But she'd seen his eyes flicker down over her bodice, scan the ripped silk that exposed flesh at her side.

She knew how to use her looks as a weapon. Deliberately she tipped her face up to his, let her eyes fill helplessly. "I'm so frightened. So alone." She risked touching a hand to his arm. "You won't hurt me, will you? Please don't hurt me. I'll do anything you want."

He said nothing, but his eyes were keen on her face when she moistened her lips with the tip of her tongue, keeping the movement slow and provocative. "Anything," she repeated, her voice husky, intimate. "You're so strong, so…in charge." Did he even speak English? she wondered. What did it matter? The communication was clear enough.

At the door to her prison, she turned, flashed a smoldering look, sighed deeply. "Don't leave me alone," she murmured. "I'm so afraid of being alone. I need… someone." Taking a chance, she lifted a fingertip, rubbed it over his lips. "He doesn't have to know," she whispered. "No one has to know. It's our secret."

Though it revolted her, she took his hand, placed it on her breast. The flex of his fingers chilled her skin, but she made herself smile invitingly as he lowered his head and crushed her mouth.

Don't think of it, don't think, she warned herself as his hands roamed her. It's not you. He's not touching you.

"Inside." She hoped he interpreted her quick shudder as desire. "Come inside with me. We'll be alone."

He opened the door, his eyes still hungry on her face, on her body. She would either win here, she thought, or lose everything. She let out a teasing laugh as he grabbed for her the moment the door was locked behind him.

"Oh, there's no hurry now, handsome." She tossed her hair back, glided out of his reach. "No need to rush such a lovely friendship. I want to freshen up for you."

Still he said nothing, but his eyes were narrowing with impatience, suspicion. Still smiling, she reached for the heavy cut-crystal atomizer on the bureau. A woman's weapon, she thought coldly as she gently spritzed her skin, the air. "I prefer using all of my senses." Her fingers tightened convulsively on the bottle as she swayed toward him.

She jerked the bottle up and sprayed perfume directly into his leering eyes. He hissed in shock, grabbed instinctively for his stinging eyes. Putting all her strength behind it, she smashed the crystal into his face, and her knee into his groin.

He staggered, but didn't go down. There was blood on his face, and beneath it, his skin had gone a pasty shade of white. He was fumbling for his gun and, frantic, she kicked out, aiming low again. This time he went to his knees, but his hands were still reaching for the gun snapped to his side.

Sobbing now, she heaved up a footstool, upholstered in white, tasseled in gold. She rammed it into his already bleeding face, then, lifting it high, crashed it onto his head. Desperately she scrabbled to unstrap his gun, her clammy hands slipping off leather and steel. When she held it in two shaking hands, prepared to do whatever was necessary, she saw that he was unconscious.

Her breath tore out of her lungs in a wild laugh. "I guess I'm just not that kind of girl." Too frightened for caution, she yanked the keys free of his clip, stabbed one after the other at the lock until it gave. And raced like a deer fleeing wolves, down the corridor, through the golden light.

A shadow moved at the head of the stairs, and with a low, keening moan, she lifted the gun.

"That's the second time you've pointed a weapon in my direction."

Her vision grayed at the sound of Seth's voice. Clamping down hard on her lip, she cleared it as he stepped out of the shadows and into the light. "You. You came."

It wasn't armor he wore, she thought dizzily. But black—shirt, slacks, shoes. It wasn't a sword he carried, but a gun.

It wasn't a memory. It was real.

Her dress was torn, bloody. Her face was bruised, her eyes were glassy with shock. He'd killed two men to get this far. And seeing her this way, he thought it hadn't been enough. Not nearly enough.

"It's all right now." He resisted the urge to rush to her, grab her close. She looked as though she might shatter at a touch. "We're going to get you out. No one's going to hurt you."

"He's going to kill them." She forced air in and out of her lungs. "He's going to kill them no matter what I do. He's insane. They're not safe from him. We're none of us safe from him. He killed you before," she ended on a whisper. "He'll try again."

He took her arm to steady her, gently slipped the gun from her hand. "Where is he, Grace?"

"There's a room, through a panel in the library, down the stairs. Just like before…lifetimes ago. Do you remember?" Spinning between images, she pressed a hand to her head. "He's there with his toys, all the glittering toys. I stabbed him with a dinner knife."

"Good girl." How much of the blood was hers? He could detect no wound other than the bruises on her face and arms. "Come on now, come with me."

He led her down the stairs. There was the guard she'd seen before. But he wasn't standing now. Averting her eyes, she stepped around him, gestured. She was steadier now. The past didn't always run in a loop, she knew. Sometimes it changed. People made it change.

"It's back there, the third door down on the left." She cringed when she caught a movement. But it was Jack, melting out of a doorway.

"It's clear," he said to Seth.

"Take her out." His eyes said everything as he

nudged her into Jack's arms. *Take care of her. I'm trusting you.*

Jack hitched her against his side to keep his weapon hand free. "You're okay, honey."

"No." She shook her head. "He's going to kill them. He has explosives, something, at the house, at the pub. You have to stop him. The panel. I'll show you."

She wrenched away from Jack, staggered like a drunk toward the library. "Here." She turned a rosette in the carving of the chair rail. "I watched him." The panel slid smoothly open.

"Jack, get her out. Call in a 911. I'll deal with him."

She was floating, just under the surface of thick, warm water. "He'll have to kill him," she said faintly as Seth disappeared into the opening. "This time he can't fail."

"He knows what he has to do."

"Yes, he always does." And the room spun once, wildly. "Jack, I'm sorry," she managed before she spun with it.

He hadn't locked the door, Seth noted. Arrogant bastard, so sure no one would trespass on his sacred ground. With his weapon lifted, Seth eased the heavy door open, blinked once at the bright gleam of gold.

He stepped inside, focused on the man sitting in

a thronelike chair in the center of all the glory. "It's done, DeVane."

DeVane wasn't surprised. He'd known the man would come. "You risk a great deal." His smile was cold as a snake's, his eyes mad as a hatter's. "You did before. You remember, don't you? Dreamed of it, didn't you? You came to steal from me before, to take the Stars and the woman. You had a sword then, heavy and unjeweled."

Something vague and quick passed through Seth's mind. A stone castle, a stormy sky, a room of great wealth. A woman beloved. On an altar, a triangle wrenched from the hands of the god, adorned with diamonds as blue as stars.

"I killed you." DeVane laughed softly. "Left your body for the crows."

"That was then." Seth stepped forward. "This is now."

DeVane's smile spread. "I am beyond you." He lifted his hand, and the gun he held in it.

Two shots were fired, so close together they sounded as one. The room shook, echoed, settled, and went back to gleaming. Slowly Seth stepped closer, looked down at the man who lay facedown on a hill of gold.

"Now you are," Seth murmured. "You're beyond me now."

She heard the shots. For one unspeakable moment

everything inside her stopped. Heart, mind, breath, blood. Then it started again, a tidal wave of feeling that had her springing off the bench where Jack had put her, the air heaving in and out of her lungs.

And she knew, because she felt, because her heart could beat, that it hadn't been Seth who'd met the bullet. If he had died, she would have known. Some piece of her heart would have broken off from the whole and shattered.

Still, she waited, her eyes on the house, because she had to see.

The stars wheeled overhead, the moon shot light through the trees. Somewhere in the distance, a night bird began to call out, with hope and joy.

Then he walked out of the house. Whole. Tears clogged her throat and were swallowed. They stung her eyes and were willed away. She had to see him clearly, the man she had accepted that she loved, and couldn't have.

He walked to her, his eyes dark and cool, his gait steady.

He'd already regained control, she realized. Already tucked whatever he'd had to do away in some compartment where it wouldn't interfere with what had to be done next.

She wrapped her arms around herself, hands clamped tight on her forearms. She'd never know that one gesture, that turning into herself and not him, was what stopped him from reaching for her.

So he stood, with an armspan of distance between them and looked at the woman he accepted that he loved, and had pushed away.

She was pale, and even now he could see the quick trembles that ripped through her. But he wouldn't have said she was fragile. Even now, with death shimmering between them, she wasn't fragile.

Her voice was strong and steady. "It's over?"

"Yeah, it's over."

"He was going to kill them."

"That's over, too." His need to touch her, to hold on, was overwhelming. He felt that his knees were about to give way. But she turned, shifted her body away, and looked out into the dark.

"I need to see them. Bailey and M.J."

"I know."

"You need my statement."

God. His control wavered enough for him to press his fingers against burning eyes. "It can wait."

"Why? I want it over. I need to put it behind me." She steadied herself again, then turned slowly. And when she faced him, his hands were at his sides and his eyes clear. "I need to put it all behind me."

Her meaning was clear enough, Seth thought. He was part of that all.

"Grace, you're hurt and you're in shock. An ambulance is on the way."

"I don't need an ambulance."

"Don't tell me what the hell you need." Fury swarmed through him, buzzed in his head like a nest of mad hornets. "I said the damn statement can wait. You're shaking. For God's sake, sit down."

When he reached out to take her arm, she jerked back, her chin snapping up, her shoulders hunching. "Don't touch me. Just...don't." If he touched her, she might break. If she broke she would weep. And weeping, she would beg.

The words were a knife in the gut, the deep and desperate blue of her eyes a blow to the face. Because he felt his fingers tremble, he stuffed them into his pockets, took a step back. "All right. Sit down. Please."

Had he thought she wasn't fragile? She looked as if she would shatter into pieces with one hard thought. She was sheet pale, her eyes enormous. Blood and bruises marked her face.

And there was nothing he could do. Nothing she would let him do.

He heard the distant wail of sirens, and footsteps from behind him. Cade, his face grim, walked to Grace, tucked a blanket he'd brought from the house over her shoulders.

Seth watched as she turned into him, how her body

seemed to go fluid and flow into the arms Cade offered her. He heard the fractured sob even as she muffled it against Cade's shoulder.

"Get her out of here." His fingers burned to reach out, stroke her hair, to take something away with him. "Get her the hell out of here."

He walked back into the house to do what needed to be done.

The birds sang their morning song as Grace stepped out into her garden. The woods were quiet and green. And safe. She'd needed to come here, to her country escape. To come alone. To be alone.

Bailey and M.J. had understood. In a few days, she thought, she would go into town, call, see if they'd like to come up, bring Jack and Cade. She would need to see them soon. But she couldn't bear to go back yet. Not yet.

She could still hear the shots, the quick jolt of them shuddering through her as Jack had taken her outside. She'd known it was DeVane and not Seth who had met the bullet. She'd simply known.

She hadn't seen Seth again that night. It had been easy to avoid him in the confusion that followed. She'd answered all the questions the local police had asked, made statements to the government officials. She'd stood up to it, then quietly demanded that Cade or Jack take her to Salvini, take her to Bailey and M.J.

And the Three Stars.

Stepping down onto her blooming terraces, she brought it back into her head, and her heart. The three of them standing in the near dark of a near-empty room, she with her torn and bloody dress.

Each of them had taken a point of the triangle, had felt the sing of power, seen the flicker of impossible light. And had known it was done.

"It's as if we've done this before," Bailey had murmured. "But it wasn't enough then. It was lost, and so were we."

"It's enough now." M.J. had looked up, met each of their eyes in turn. "Like a cycle, complete. A chain, with the links forged. It's weird, but it's right."

"A museum instead of a temple this time." Regret and relief had mixed within Grace as they set the Stars down again. "A promise kept, and, I suppose, destinies fulfilled."

She'd turned to both of them, embraced them. Another triangle. "I've always loved you both, needed you both. Can we go somewhere? The three of us." The tears had come then, flooding. "I need to talk."

She'd told them everything, poured out heart and soul, hurt and terror, until she was empty. And she supposed, because it was them, she'd healed a little.

Now she would heal on her own.

She could do it here, Grace knew, and, closing her eyes, she just breathed. Then, because it always soothed, she set down her gardening basket, and began to tend her blooms.

She heard the car coming, the rumble of wheels on gravel, and her brow creased in mild irritation. Her neighbors were few and far between and rarely intruded. She wanted no company but her plants, and she stood, her flowers flowing at her feet, determined to politely and firmly send the visitor away again.

Her heart kicked once, hard, when she saw that the car was Seth's. She watched in silence as it stopped in the middle of her lane and he got out and started toward her.

She looked like something out of a misty legend herself, he thought. Her hair blowing in the breeze, the long, loose skirt of her dress fluttering, and flowers in a sea around her. His nerves jangled.

And his stomach clutched when he saw the bruise marring her cheek.

"You're a long way from home, Seth." She spoke without expression as he stopped two steps beneath her.

"You're a hard woman to find, Grace."

"That's the way I prefer it. I don't care for company here."

"Obviously." Both to give himself time to settle and

because he was curious, he scanned the land, the house perched on the hill, the deep secrets of the woods. "It's a beautiful spot."

"Yes."

"Remote." His gaze shifted back to hers so quickly, so intensely, he nearly made her jolt. "Peaceful. You've earned some peace."

"That's why I'm here." She lifted a brow. "And why are you here?"

"I needed to talk to you. Grace—"

"I intended to see you when I came back," she said quickly. "We didn't talk much that night. I suppose I was more shaken up than I realized. I never even thanked you."

It was worse, he realized, that cool, polite voice was worse than a shouted curse. "You don't have anything to thank me for."

"You saved my life and, I believe, the lives of the people I love. I know you broke rules, even the law, to find me, to get me away from him. I'm grateful."

The palms of his hands went clammy. She was making him see it again, feel it again. All that rage and terror. "I'd have done anything to get you away from him."

"Yes, I think I know that." She had to look away. It hurt too much to look into his eyes. She'd promised herself, sworn to herself she wouldn't be hurt again.

"And I wonder if any of us had a choice in what happened over that short, intense period of time. Or," she added with a ghost of a smile, "if you choose to believe what happened, over centuries. I hope you haven't—that your career won't suffer because of what you did for me."

His eyes went dark, flat. "The job's secure, Grace."

"I'm glad." He had to leave, she thought. He had to leave now, before she crumbled. "I still intend to write a letter to your superiors. And you might know I have an uncle in the Senate. I wouldn't be surprised, when the smoke clears, if you got a promotion out of it."

His throat was raw. He couldn't clear it. "Look at me, damn it." When her gaze shot back to his face, he curled his hands into fists to keep from touching her. "Do you think that matters?"

"Yes, I do. It matters, Seth, certainly to me. But for now, I'm taking a few days, so if you'll excuse me, I want to get to my gardening before the heat of the day."

"Do you think this ends it?"

She leaned over, took up her clippers and snipped off wilted blooms. They faded all too quickly, she thought. And that left an ache in the heart. "I think you already ended it."

"Don't turn away from me." He took her arm, hauled her toward him, as panic and fury spiraled through him. "You can't just turn away. I can't—" He broke off, his hand lifting to lie on the bruise on her cheek. "Oh, God, Grace. He hurt you."

"It's nothing." She stepped back quickly, nearly flinching, and his hand fell heavily to his side. "Bruises fade. And he's gone. You saw to that. He's gone, and it's over. The Three Stars are where they belong, and everything's back in its place. Everything's as it was meant to be."

"Is it?" He didn't step to her, couldn't bear to see her shrink back from him again. "I hurt you, and you won't forgive me for it."

"Not entirely," she agreed, fighting to keep it light. "But saving my life goes a long way to—"

"Stop it," he said in a voice both ragged and quiet. "Just stop it." Undone, he whirled away, pacing, nearly trampling her bedding plants. He hadn't known he could suffer like this—the ice in the belly, the heat in the brain.

He spoke, looking out into her woods, into shadows and cool green shade. "Do you know what it did to me, knowing he had you? Knowing it. Hearing your voice on the phone, the fear in it?"

"I don't want to think about it. I don't want to think about any of that."

"I can't do anything but think of it. And see you— every time I close my eyes, I see you the way you stood there in that hallway, blood on your dress, marks on your skin. Not knowing—not knowing what he'd done to you. And remembering—half remembering some other time when I couldn't stop him."

"It's over," she said again, because her legs were turning to water. "Leave it alone."

"You might have gotten away without me," he continued. "You took out a guard twice your size. You might have pulled it off without any help from me. You might not have needed me at all. And I realized that was part of my problem all along. Believing, being certain, I needed you so much more than you could possibly need me. Being afraid of that. Stupid to be afraid of that," he said as he came up the steps again. "Once you understand real fear, the fear of knowing you could lose the most important thing in your life in one single heartbeat, nothing else can touch you."

He gathered her to him, too desperate to heed her resistance. And, with a shuddering gulp of air, buried his face in her hair. "Don't push me away, don't send me away."

"This isn't any good." It hurt to be held by him, yet she wished she could go on being held just like this, with the sun warm on her skin and his face pressed into her hair.

"I need you. I need you," he repeated, and turned his urgent mouth to hers.

The hammer blow of emotion struck and she buckled. It swirled from one of them to the other in an unbridled storm, left her heart shaken and weak. She closed her eyes, slid her arms around him. Need would be enough, she promised herself. She would make it enough for both of them. There was too much inside her that she ached to give for her to turn him away.

"I won't send you away." Her hands stroked over his back, soothed the tension. "I'm glad you're here. I want you here." She drew back, brought his hand to her cheek. "Come inside, Seth. Come to bed."

His fingers tightened on hers. Then gently lifted her head up. It made him ache to realize she believed there was only that he wanted from her. That he'd let her think it.

"Grace, I didn't come here to take you to bed. I didn't come here to start where we left off."

Why had he been so resistant to seeing what was in her eyes? he wondered. Why had he refused to believe what was so blatantly real, so generously offered to him.

"I came here to beg. The third Star is generosity," he said, almost to himself. "You didn't make me beg. I didn't come here for sex, Grace. Or for gratitude."

Confused, she shook her head. "What do you want, Seth? Why did you come?"

He wasn't sure he'd fully realized why until just now. "To hear you tell me what you want. What you need."

"Peace." She gestured. "I have that here. Friendship. I have that, too."

"And that's it? That's enough?"

"It's been enough all my life."

He caught her face in his hands before she could step away. "If you could have more? What do you want, Grace?"

"Wanting what you can't have only makes you unhappy."

"Tell me." He kept his eyes focussed on hers. "Straight out, for once. Just say what you want."

"Family. Children. I want children and a man who loves me—who wants to make that family with me." Her lips curved slowly, but the smile didn't reach her eyes. "Surprised I'd want to spoil my figure? Spend a few years of my life changing diapers?"

"No." He slid his hands down to her shoulders, firming his grip. She was poised to move, he noted. To run. "No, I'm not surprised."

"Really? Well." She moved her shoulders as if to shrug off the weight of his touch. "If you're going to stay, let's go inside. I'm thirsty."

"Grace, I love you." He watched her smile slide away from her face, felt her body go absolutely still.

"What? What did you say to me?"

"I love you." Saying it, he realized, was power. True power. "I fell in love with you before I'd seen you. Fell in love with an image, a memory, a wish. I can't be sure which it is, or if it was all of them. I don't know if it was fate, or choice, or luck. But it was so fast, so hard, so deep, I wouldn't let myself believe, and I wouldn't let myself trust. And I turned you away because you let yourself do both. I came here to tell you that." His hands slid down her arms and clasped hers.

"Grace, I'm asking you to believe in us again, to trust in us again. And to marry me."

"You—" She had to take a step back, had to press a hand to her heart. "You want to marry me."

"I'm asking you to come back with me today. I know it's old-fashioned, but I want you to meet my family."

The pressure in her chest all but burst her heart. "You want me to meet your family."

"I want them to meet the woman I love, the woman I want to have a life with. The life I've been waiting to start—waiting for her to start." He brought her hand to his cheek, held it there while his eyes looked deep into hers. "The woman I want to make children with."

"Oh." The weight on her chest released in a flood, poured out of her…until her heart was in her swimming eyes.

"Don't cry." It seemed he would beg after all. "Grace, please, don't. Don't tell me I left it too late." Awkwardly he brushed at her tears with his thumbs. "Don't tell me I ruined it."

"I love you so much." She closed her fingers around his wrists, watched the emotion leap into his eyes. "I've been so unhappy waiting for you. I was so sure I'd missed you. Again. Somehow."

"Not this time." He kept his hands on her face, kissed her gently. "Not ever again."

"No, not ever again," she murmured against his lips.

"Say yes," he asked her. "I want to hear you say yes."

"Yes. To everything."

She held him close in the flower-scented morning where the stars slept behind the sky. And felt the last link of an endless chain fall into place.

"Seth."

He kept his eyes shut, his cheek on her hair. And his smile bloomed slow and easy. "Grace."

"We're where we're supposed to be. Can you feel it?" She drew a deep breath. "All of us are where we belong now."

She lifted her face, found his mouth waiting. "And now," he said quietly, "it begins."

* * * * *

Please read on for a taster of **Long Summer Days** by *New York Times* bestselling author Nora Roberts, a collection of two fabulous summery romances – *Treasures Lost, Treasures Found* and *Temptation* – perfect beach reading!

Long Summer Days is available in June 2017.

Don't miss it!

Chapter 1

He had believed in it. Edwin J. Hardesty hadn't been
the kind of man who had fantasies or followed dreams,
but sometime during his quiet, literary life he had
looked for a pot of gold. From the information in the
reams of notes, the careful charts and the dog-eared
research books, he thought he'd found it.

In the panelled study, a single light shot a beam
across a durable oak desk. The light fell over a hand—
narrow, slender, without the affectation of rings or polish. Yet even bare, it remained an essentially feminine
hand, the kind that could be pictured holding a porcelain cup or waving a feather fan. It was a surprisingly
elegant hand for a woman who didn't consider herself elegant, delicate or particularly feminine. Kathleen Hardesty was, as her father had been, and as he'd
directed her to be, a dedicated educator.

Minds were her concern—the expanding and the fulfilling of them. This included her own as well as every one of her students'. For as long as she could remember, her father had impressed upon her the importance of education. He'd stressed the priority of it over every other aspect of life. Education was the cohesiveness that held civilization together. She grew up surrounded by the dusty smell of books and the quiet, placid tone of patient instruction.

She'd been expected to excel in school, and she had. She'd been expected to follow her father's path into education. At twenty-eight, Kate was just finishing her first year at Yale as an assistant professor of English literature.

In the dim light of the quiet study, she looked the part. Her light brown hair was tidily secured at the nape of her neck with all the pins neatly tucked in. Her practical tortoiseshell reading glasses seemed dark against her milk-pale complexion. Her high cheekbones gave her face an almost haughty look that was often dispelled by her warm, doe-brown eyes.

Though her jacket was draped over the back of her chair, the white blouse she wore was still crisp. Her cuffs were turned back to reveal delicate wrists and a slim Swiss watch on her left arm. Her earrings were tasteful gold studs given to Kate by her father on her twenty-first birthday, the only truly personal gift she could ever remember receiving from him.

Seven long years later, one short week after her father's funeral, Kate sat at his desk. The room still carried the scent of his cologne and a hint of the pipe tobacco he'd only smoked in that room.

She'd finally found the courage to go through his papers.

She hadn't known he was ill. In his early sixties, Hardesty had looked robust and strong. He hadn't told his daughter about his visits to the doctor, his check-ups, ECG results or the little pills he carried with him everywhere. She'd found his pills in his inside pocket after his fatal heart attack. Kate hadn't known his heart was weak because Hardesty never shared his shortcomings with anyone. She hadn't known about the charts and research papers in his desk; he'd never shared his dreams either.

Now that she was aware of both, Kate wasn't certain she ever really knew the man who'd raised her. The memory of her mother was dim; that was to be expected after more than twenty years. Her father had been alive just a week before.

Leaning back for a moment, she pushed her glasses up and rubbed the bridge of her nose between her thumb and forefinger. She tried, with only the desk lamp between herself and the dark, to think of her father in precise terms.

Physically, he'd been a tall, big man with a full head of steel-gray hair and a patient face. He had favored dark suits and white shirts. The only vanity she could remember had been his weekly manicures. But it wasn't a physical picture Kate struggled with now. As a father...

He was never unkind. In all her memories, Kate couldn't remember her father ever raising his voice to her, ever striking her. He never had to, she thought with a sigh. All he had to do was express disappointment, disapproval, and that was enough.

He had been brilliant, tireless, dedicated. But all of that had been directed toward his vocation. As a father, Kate reflected… He'd never been unkind. That was all that would come to her, and because of it she felt a fresh wave of guilt and grief.

She hadn't disappointed him, that much she could cling to. He had told her so himself, in just those words, when she was accepted by the English Department at Yale. Nor had he expected her ever to disappoint him. Kate knew, though it had never been discussed, that her father wanted her to become head of the English Department within ten years. That had been the extent of his dream for her.

Had he ever realized just how much she'd loved him? She wondered as she shut her eyes, tired now from the hours of reading her father's handwriting. Had he ever known just how desperately she'd wanted to please him? If he'd just once said he was proud…

In the end, she hadn't had those few intense last moments with her father one reads about in books or sees in the movies. When she'd arrived at the hospital, he was already gone. There'd been no time for words. No time for tears.

Now she was on her own in the tidy Cape Cod house she'd shared with him for so long. The housekeeper would still come on Wednesday mornings, and the gardener would come on Saturdays to cut the grass. She alone would have to deal with the paperwork, the sorting, the shifting, the clearing out.

That could be done. Kate leaned back farther in her father's worn leather chair. It could be done because all of those things were practical matters. She dealt easily with the practical. But what about these papers she'd found? What would she do about the carefully drawn charts, the notebooks filled with information, directions, history, theory? In part, because she was raised to be logical, she considered filing them neatly away.

But there was another part, the part that enabled one to lose oneself in fantasies, in dreams, in the "perhapses" of life. This was the part that allowed Kate to lose herself totally in the possibilities of the written word, in the wonders of a book. The papers on her father's desk beckoned her.

He'd believed in it. She bent over the papers again. He'd believed in it or he never would have wasted his time documenting, searching, theorizing. She would never be able to discuss it with him. Yet, in a way, wasn't he telling her about it through his words?

Treasure. Sunken treasure. The stuff of fiction and Hollywood movies. Judging by the stack of papers and notebooks on his desk, Hardesty must have spent months, perhaps years, compiling information on the location of an English merchant ship lost off the coast of North Carolina two centuries before.

It brought Kate an immediate picture of Edward Teach—Blackbeard, the bloodthirsty pirate with the crazed superstitions and reign of terror. The stuff of romances, she thought. Of romance…

Ocracoke Island. The memory was sharp, sweet and painful. Kate had blocked out everything that had hap-

pened that summer four years before. Everything and
everyone. Now, if she was to make a rational decision
about what was to be done, she had to think of those
long, lazy months on the remote Outer Banks of North
Carolina.

She'd begun work on her doctorate. It had been a surprise when her father had announced that he planned
to spend the summer on Ocracoke and invited her to
accompany him. Of course, she'd gone, taking her por-
table typewriter, boxes of books, reams of paper. She
hadn't expected to be seduced by white sand beaches
and the call of gulls. She hadn't expected to fall desperately and insensibly in love.

Insensibly, Kate repeated to herself, as if in defense.
She'd have to remember that was the most apt adjec-
tive. There'd been nothing sensible about her feelings
for Ky Silver.

Even the name, she mused, was unique, unconven-
tional, flashy. They'd been as suitable for each other
as a peacock and a wren. Yet that hadn't stopped her
from losing her head, her heart and her innocence during that balmy, magic summer.

She could still see him at the helm of the boat her
father had rented, steering into the wind, laughing,
dark hair flowing wildly. She could still remember
that heady, weightless feeling when they'd gone scuba
diving in the warm coastal waters. Kate had been too
caught up in what was happening to herself to think
about her father's sudden interest in boating and diving.

She'd been too swept away by her own feelings of
astonishment that a man like Ky Silver should be at-

tracted to someone like her to notice her father's pre-occupation with currents and tides. There'd been too much excitement for her to realize that her father never bothered with fishing rods like the other vacationers.

But now her youthful fancies were behind her, Kate told herself. Now, she could clearly remember how many hours her father had closeted himself in his hotel room, reading book after book that he brought with him from the mainland library. He'd been researching even then. She was sure he'd continued that research in the following summers when she had refused to go back. Refused to go back, Kate remembered, because of Ky Silver.

Ky had asked her to believe in fairy tales. He asked her to give him the impossible. When she refused, frightened, he shrugged and walked away without a second look. She had never gone back to the white sand and gulls since then.

Kate looked down again at her father's papers. She had to go back now—go back and finish what her father had started. Perhaps, more than the house, the trust fund, the antique jewelry that had been her mother's, this was her father's legacy to her. If she filed those papers neatly away, they'd haunt her for the rest of her life.

She had to go back, Kate reaffirmed as she took off her glasses and folded them neatly on the blotter. And it was Ky Silver she'd have to go to. Her father's aspirations had drawn her away from Ky once; now, four years later, they were drawing her back.

But Dr. Kathleen Hardesty knew the difference between fairy tales and reality. Reaching in her father's desk drawer, she drew out a sheet of thick creamy stationery and began to write.

Ky let the wind buffet him as he opened the throttle. He liked speed in much the same way he liked a lazy afternoon in the hammock. They were two of the things that made life worthwhile. He was used to the smell of salt spray, but he still inhaled deeply. He was well accustomed to the vibration of the deck under his feet, but he still felt it. He wasn't a man to let anything go unnoticed or unappreciated.

He grew up in this quiet, remote little coastal town, and though he'd traveled and intended to travel more, he didn't plan to live anywhere else. It suited him—the freedom of the sea, and the coziness of a small community.

He didn't resent the tourists because he knew they helped keep the village alive, but he preferred the island in winter. Then the storms blew wild and cold, and only the hearty would brave the ferry across Hatteras Inlet.

He fished, but unlike the majority of his neighbors, he rarely sold what he caught. What he pulled out of the sea, he ate. He dove, occasionally collecting shells, but again, this was for his own pleasure. Often he took tourists out on his boat to fish or to scuba dive, because there were times he enjoyed the company. But there were afternoons, like this sparkling one, when he simply wanted the sea to himself.

He had always been restless. His mother had said that he came into the world two weeks early because he grew impatient waiting. Ky turned thirty-two that spring, but was far from settled. He knew what he wanted—to live as he chose. The trouble was that he wasn't certain just what he wanted to choose.

At the moment, he chose the open sky and the endless sea. There were other moments when he knew that that wouldn't be enough.

But the sun was hot, the breeze cool and the shoreline was drawing near. The boat's motor was purring smoothly and in the small cooler was a tidy catch of fish he'd cook up for his supper that night. On a crystal, sparkling afternoon, perhaps it was enough.

From the shore he looked like a pirate might if there were pirates in the twentieth century. His hair was long enough to curl over his ears and well over the collar of a shirt had he worn one. It was black, a rich, true black that might have come from his Arapaho or Sicilian blood. His eyes were the deep, dark green of the sea on a cloudy day. His skin was bronzed from years in the sun, taut from the years of swimming and pulling in nets. His bone structure was also part of his heritage, sculpted, hard, defined.

When he smiled as he did now, racing the wind to shore, his face took on that reckless freedom women found irresistible. When he didn't smile, his eyes could turn as cold as a lion's before a leap. He discovered long ago that women found that equally irresistible.

Ky drew back on the throttle so that the boat slowed, rocked, then glided into its slip in Silver Lake Harbor. With the quick, efficient movements of one born to the sea, he leaped onto the dock to secure the lines.

"Catch anything?"

Ky straightened and turned. He smiled, but absently, as one does at a brother seen almost every day of one's life. "Enough. Things slow at the Roost?"

Marsh smiled, and there was a brief flicker of family resemblance, but his eyes were a calm light brown and his hair was carefully styled. "Worried about your investment?"

Ky gave a half-shrug. "With you running things?"

Marsh didn't comment. They knew each other as intimately as men ever know each other. One was restless, the other calm. The opposition never seemed to matter. "Linda wants you to come up for dinner. She worries about you."

She would, Ky thought, amused. His sister-in-law loved to mother and fuss, even though she was five years younger than Ky. That was one of the reasons the restaurant she ran with Marsh was such a success— that, plus Marsh's business sense and the hefty investment and shrewd renovations Ky had made. Ky left the managing up to his brother and his sister-in-law. He didn't mind owning a restaurant, even keeping half an eye on the profit and loss, but he certainly had no interest in running one.

After the lines were secure, he wiped his palms down the hips of his cut-offs. "What's the special tonight?"

Marsh dipped his hands into his front pockets and rocked back on his heels. "Bluefish."

Grinning, Ky tossed back the lid of his cooler revealing his catch. "Tell Linda not to worry. I'll eat."

"That's not going to satisfy her." Marsh glanced at

his brother as Ky looked out to sea. "She thinks you're alone too much."

"You're only alone too much if you don't like being alone." Ky glanced back over his shoulder. He didn't want to debate now, when the exhilaration of the speed and the sea were still upon him. But he'd never been a man to placate. "Maybe you two should think about having another baby, then Linda would be too busy to worry about big brothers."

"Give me a break. Hope's only eighteen months old."

"You've got to add nine to that," Ky reminded him carelessly. He was fond of his niece, despite—no, because she was a demon. "Anyway, it looks like the family lineage is in your hands."

"Yeah." Marsh shifted his feet, cleared his throat and fell silent. It was a habit he'd carried since childhood, one that could annoy or amuse Ky depending on his mood. At the moment, it was only mildly distracting.

Something was in the air. He could smell it, but he couldn't quite identify it. A storm brewing, he wondered? One of those hot, patient storms that seemed capable of brewing for weeks. He was certain he could smell it.

"Why don't you tell me what else is on your mind?" Ky suggested. "I want to get back to the house and clean these."

"You had a letter. It was put in our box by mistake."

It was a common enough occurrence, but by his brother's expression Ky knew there was more. His sense of an impending storm grew sharper. Saying nothing, he held out his hand.

"Ky..." Marsh began. There was nothing he could say, just as there'd been nothing to say four years before. Reaching in his back pocket, he drew out the letter.

The envelope was made from heavy cream-colored paper. Ky didn't have to look at the return address. The handwriting and the memories it brought leaped out at him. For a moment, he felt his breath catch in his lungs as it might if someone had caught him with a blow to the solar plexus. Deliberately, he expelled it. "Thanks," he said, as if it meant nothing. He stuck the letter in his pocket before he picked up his cooler and gear.

"Ky—" Again Marsh broke off. His brother had turned his head, and the cool, half-impatient stare said very clearly—back off. "If you change your mind about dinner," Marsh said.

"I'll let you know." Ky went down the length of the dock without looking back.

He was grateful he hadn't bothered to bring his car down to the harbor. He needed to walk. He needed the fresh air and the exercise to keep his mind clear while he remembered what he didn't want to remember. What he never really forgot.

Kate. Four years ago she'd walked out of his life with the same sort of cool precision with which she'd walked into it. She had reminded him of a Victorian doll—a little prim, a little aloof. He'd never had much patience with neatly folded hands or haughty manners, yet almost from the first instant he'd wanted her.

At first, he thought it was the fact that she was so different. A challenge—something for Ky Silver to conquer. He enjoyed teaching her to dive, and watching the precise step-by-step way she learned. It hadn't been any hardship to look at her in a snug scuba suit, although she didn't have voluptuous curves. She had a trim, neat, almost boylike figure and what seemed like yards of thick, soft hair.

He could still remember the first time she took it down from its pristine knot. It left him breathless, hurting, fascinated. Ky would have touched it—touched her then and there if her father hadn't been standing beside her. But if a man was clever, if a man was determined, he could find a way to be alone with a woman.

Ky had found ways. Kate had taken to diving as though she'd been born to it. While her father had buried himself in his books, Ky had taken Kate out on the water—under the water, to the silent, dreamlike world that had attracted her just as it had always attracted him.

He could remember the first time he kissed her. They had been wet and cool from a dive, standing on the deck of his boat. He was able to see the lighthouse behind her and the vague line of the coast. Her hair had flowed down her back, sleek from the water, dripping with it. He'd reached out and gathered it in his hand.

"What are you doing?"

Four years later, he could hear that low, cultured, eastern voice, the curiosity in it. It took no effort for him to see the curiosity that had been in her eyes.

"I'm going to kiss you."

The curiosity had remained in her eyes, fascinating him. "Why?"

"Because I want to."

It was as simple as that for him. He wanted to. Her body had stiffened as he'd drawn her against him. When her lips parted in protest, he closed his over them. In the time it takes a heart to beat, the rigidity had melted from her body. She'd kissed him with all the young, stored-up passion that had been in her—passion mixed with innocence. He was experienced enough to recognize her innocence, and that too had fascinated him. Ky had, foolishly, youthfully and completely, fallen in love.

Kate had remained an enigma to him, though they shared impassioned hours of laughter and long, lazy talks. He admired her thirst for learning and she had a predilection for putting knowledge into neat slots that baffled him. She was enthusiastic about diving, but it hadn't been enough for her simply to be able to swim freely underwater, taking her air from tanks. She had to know how the tanks worked, why they were fashioned a certain way. Ky watched her absorb what he told her, and knew she'd retain it.

They had taken walks along the shoreline at night and she had recited poetry from memory. Beautiful words, Byron, Shelley, Keats. And he, who'd never been overly impressed by such things, had eaten it up because her voice had made the words somehow personal. Then she'd begin to talk about syntax, iambic pentameters, and Ky would find new ways to divert her.

For three months, he did little but think of her. For the first time, Ky had considered changing his lifestyle. His little cottage near the beach needed work. It needed furniture. Kate would need more than milk crates and the hammock that had been his style. Because he'd been young and had never been in love before, Ky had taken his own plans for granted.

She'd walked out on him. She'd had her own plans, and he hadn't been part of them.

Her father came back to the island the following summer, and every summer thereafter. Kate never came back. Ky knew she had completed her doctorate and was teaching in a prestigious ivy league school where her father was all but a cornerstone. She had what she wanted. So, he told himself as he swung open the screen door of his cottage, did he. He went where he wanted, when he wanted. He called his own shots. His responsibilities extended only as far as he chose to extend them. To his way of thinking, that itself was a mark of success.

Setting the cooler on the kitchen floor, Ky opened the refrigerator. He twisted the top off a beer and drank half of it in one icy cold swallow. It washed some of the bitterness out of his mouth.

Calm now, and curious, he pulled the letter out of his pocket. Ripping it open, he drew out the single neatly written sheet.

Dear Ky,
You may or may not be aware that my father suffered a fatal heart attack two weeks ago. It was very sudden, and I'm currently trying to tie up the many details this involves.

In going through my father's papers, I find that he had again made arrangements to come to the island this summer, and engage your services. I now find it necessary to take his place. For reasons which I'd rather explain in person, I need your help. You have my father's deposit. When I arrive in Ocracoke on the fifteenth, we can discuss terms.

If possible, contact me at the hotel, or leave a message. I hope we'll be able to come to a mutually agreeable arrangement. Please give my best to Marsh. Perhaps I'll see him during my stay.

Best,
Kathleen Hardesty

So the old man was dead. Ky set down the letter and lifted his beer again. He couldn't say he'd had any liking for Edwin Hardesty. Kate's father had been a stringent, humorless man. Still, he hadn't disliked him. Ky had, in an odd way, gotten used to his company over the last few summers. But this summer, it would be Kate.

Ky glanced at the letter again, then jogged his memory until he remembered the date. Two days, he mused. She'd be there in two days...to discuss terms. A smile played around the corners of his mouth but it didn't have anything to do with humor. They'd discuss terms, he agreed silently as he scanned Kate's letter again.

She wanted to take her father's place. Ky wondered if she'd realized, when she wrote that, just how ironic it was. Kathleen Hardesty had been obediently dogging her father's footsteps all her life. Why should that change after his death?

Had she changed? Ky wondered briefly. Would that fascinating aura of innocence and aloofness still cling to her? Or perhaps that had faded with the years. Would that rather sweet primness have developed into a rigidity? He'd see for himself in a couple of days, he realized, but tossed the letter onto the counter rather than into the trash.

So, she wanted to engage his services, he mused. Leaning both hands on either side of the sink, he looked out the window in the direction of the water he could smell, but not quite see. She wanted a business arrangement—the rental of his boat, his gear and his time. He felt the bitterness well up and swallowed it as cleanly as he had the beer. She'd have her business arrangement. And she'd pay. He'd see to that.

Ky left the kitchen with his catch still in the cooler. The appetite he'd worked up with salt spray and speed had vanished.

Treasures Lost, Treasures Found © Nora Roberts 1986